Zündel's
Exit

Zündel's Exit

Markus Werner

Translated and with a foreword by
Michael Hofmann

DALKEY ARCHIVE PRESS
CHAMPAIGN / LONDON / DUBLIN

Originally published in German as *Zündels Abgang* by Residenz Verlag,
Salzburg and Vienna, 1984

Library of Congress Cataloging-in-Publication Data

Werner, Markus.
[Zündels Abgang. English]
Zündel's Exit / Markus Werner ; translated and with a foreword by Michael Hofmann.
-- First edition.
pages cm. -- (Swiss Literature Series)
ISBN 978-1-56478-921-1 (alk. paper)
I. Hofmann, Michael, 1957 August 25- translator. II. Title.
PT2685.E6736Z8613 2013
833'.914--dc23
2013040744

Partially funded by grants from the Illinois Arts Council, a state agency, the Swiss Arts
Council Pro Helvetia, and UBS Culture Foundation

swiss arts council

pr☉helvetia

www.dalkeyarchive.com

Cover: design and composition by Mikhail Iliatov

Printed on permanent/durable acid-free paper

A rather obvious and easily accessible source—one could call it classic, were it not that it is humanly fallible and hasn't actually been in existence all that long—gives the following information about the Swiss writer Markus Werner: born in 1944, in Eschlikon, on December 27. In 1948, he moved to the canton of Schaffhausen, where he still lives. In 1974 he took his doctorate (with a thesis on Max Frisch), and joined the teaching profession. Until 1990, he worked as a teacher, at which point he gave up to write full time. He has written seven novels to date, three before that caesura, and four after, nicely spaced out (until recently) at the rate of three per decennium: *Zündels Abgang* (1984), *Froschnacht* (1985), *Die kalte Schulter* (1989), *Bis bald* (1992), *Festland* (1996), *Der ägyptische Heinrich* (1999), and *Am Hang* (2004). The last of these was the first to be translated into English, in 2012, by Robert Goodwin as *On the Edge*. The book you are holding is indeed the first of them—not that it feels or reads at all like a first novel, so assured is it (to adopt sporting parlance) of its power and pace: so distinctive, original, and fearless.

I am sorry to say I have not met Herr Werner; nor am I privy to restricted information about him, or gifted with expert opinions either. I am, however, a passionate admirer of all his books. Sometime in the late 1990s, I attended a literary festival in my home town of Freiburg; while there, I took it into my head to ask the leading German literary critic, Helmut Böttiger, also a guest at the festival (and an old Freiburg hand), for a suggestion of what or whom to read in the current German scene. Markus Werner, he said, without the smallest hesitation. I took him up on it, and bought *dtv* paperbacks of all Werner's books. They were all short, all quick, all delicious. I was by turns, and in a way that it seems only Werner knows how to produce, gripped, shaken, and rolling about with laughter. (And later, when *Am Hang* came out, I of course read that as well, in case you think I considered I had done enough, and called it quits. Not a bit of it: for me the world would always be improved by another Markus Werner novel, though, sadly, it seems doubtful whether any more will be forthcoming.) One November, I nominated one of them as my "Book of the Year" in the *Times Literary Supplement*—I have a feeling it was *Die kalte Schulter*. Years later, Aaron Kerner, during his all-too-brief stint as an assistant editor at Dalkey Archive, providentially remembered this, and asked me if I might be interested in translating a book of Werner's. Reader, I bit his hand off.

It is in the literature of small countries that one learns that life is impossible. In big countries they don't tell you such things— American writers don't, Chinese and Indian and Brazilian writers I think don't, even Russian writers don't. But this criticism of life is what you get from small European countries: Austria, Switzerland, Hungary, Poland, Ireland, Bosnia, Czechoslovakia. If it were a religion, Beckett (or in other versions, Musil or Walser or Kafka) would be its Holy Ghost, and Bernhard its God the Father, and Elfriede Jelinek or Herta Müller its Son. It is what you get when you read Bohumil Hrabal or Tadeusz Konwicki or Imre Kertesz, or *In the Hold*, or the poems of Valzhyna Mort. It is in this cult and company that Markus Werner belongs. Without clamor or fuss, he shows how the world takes a person—say Zündel here (the word suggests a spark or fuse, or match)—and calmly, callously dinches him, extinguishes him, squeezes him out, extrudes him. In form, it is like the unpredictable counter-cyclical wandering of a roulette ball, except that, instead of winding up in a little numbered pen, it goes down the drain.

Zündel's Exit is a remarkable splicing of farce and reflection, tragedy and humoresque. It is at once the tooth dropping out of a man's mouth—as if it wanted a change of scene, perhaps, or is it a cry for help?—and desperate sequences of thinking that feel like oar-strokes in a concrete boat: Zündel on the military, Zündel on gender wars, Zündel on friendship and love. It is a novel of drastic movement and intricacy, of short sentences, it struck me, with long words. Werner has an alertness toward the horror of contemporary language that in German is matched only in the poems of Hans Magnus Enzensberger. He writes, as I would put it, "facing the language"—his character, Zündel, is forever upset by speech, so that a newspaper is torture to him— and yet his novels still manage to be books of action as much as contemplation, packed with real incident and real intrigue. I can't wait for this translation to appear, so that I can sit down with friends, and—like a card game without cards—swap scenes with them: the finger in the toilet; the prostitute in Genoa; the snoozing officers; Zündel and his clerical friend Busch, our narrator, and his disdainful Vroni; Zündel and Nounou in Rapallo, both cast as products, he as noodles, she as evaporated milk. *Zündel's Exit* is a short novel that is all highlights, all climactic scenes, and yet loose enough to accommodate what the Russians deprecatingly called "philosophizing."

There is dandyishness in Zündel, as there is in all Werner's heroes and books, but it is a kind of impersonal dandyishness. He isn't a show-off—nor is his author—it's that he's complicated, and believes in the morality of complication, of sensitivity, of unpredictable and detailed responses. "*Non [. . .] come bruti*," it says in Dante. Zündel's is the tragic drama of the highly evolved, the uncontemporary, the thoughtful, the delicate, the unlikely, the mechanism of a Swiss watch—using the term put to me by Ursula Krechel—encountering the steamroller of our leveling age.

Michael Hofmann

"There were no grounds for any particular display of warmth."
—*Robert Walser*

1.

Joyous department store childhood. The only familiar presence gone AWOL in the neon aisles. The little fellow wailing inconsolably: Mama, Mama. As ever, no shortage of well-intentioned strangers, all shaken off by the child who runs around bawling. Is heard finally in another part of the forest: and here she comes, Mama, the little boy running toward her with flushed, tear-stained face and expression of relief, and she drops to her knees in front of him and spreads her arms, and, left right, left right, smacks him, and hisses, and scolds.

And Zündel? Zündel hard by, watching like the others, seeing the child gulp and go pale and start to retch. The spic and span floor. Already Mama's hands have re-fashioned themselves to retain the violet spew. There she stands, cupping them, looking forlornly about her, and the witnesses, appalled, sniffing, turn away. The cue for Zündel to jump up, offer his empty plastic carrier bag. Into which the sluggish mess of vomit slithers.

A traitor is what I am, an onlooker twiddling his thumbs. Base. Yes, I acted, true, I did something, the wrong thing and too late. Stood by that mother in her hour of need: helped her to wipe away the traces of her deed, which stink to high heaven. Good God, who wouldn't have done that in my place, sacrificed a plastic bag, a simple reflex! Does a spontaneous action deserve such lynx-eyed scrutiny, O gallant assistant? Yes, always. Onlookers: we don't like to get our hands dirty, but we pass the towel to the butcher, afterward. We don't stir while the ax is being swung. Prick up your ears: that click? Nothing. Why? Oh, we might get hurt, I mean to say. Quite, thought Zündel, rolled onto his belly, felt shame, went to sleep.

Awoke after midnight. Sobbing from next door. A man's calm voice. The sobbing stops. Instead, the wardrobe against the wall beside Zündel's bed starts to vibrate. Zündel thinks: it's always one thing or another, isn't it? Listens in spite of himself – Si si, amore, dai, dai, dai! the woman keens, then silence in the hotel again.

But by now Zündel was awake, turned on the light, stood up and inspected his face in the tiny mirror over the sink. I'm a vain fellow, he thought, but I really don't like myself. I want to leave a sign of my occupation in this room, a hidden one. He took down a picture of the Virgin Mary, and wrote on the back: It is better to be a human being dissatisfied than a pig satisfied. J.S. Mill, 1861.

All this was in Ancona, Italy.

Twenty minutes before the departure of the Ancona-Patras ferry, Zündel lost his pin-tooth (or first broad incisor.) He had just stepped inside the cramped little cabin, sheepishly asked the two men seated on one of the lower bunks where they were from (in English: Where do you come from?), and before they could give him an answer, the tooth fell out of his mouth and landed on the floor. Consternation, horror, and shame flooded Zündel. – From Bümplitz near Bern, Switzerland, the two men said simultaneously, as if – in view of his calamity – he cared the least bit about the accuracy of their reply. He managed to nod appreciatively, even though he himself was hardly Japanese, but Swiss like them, then thought: I'm damned if I'm going anywhere with a gap in my teeth.

Shortly afterward, the ferry puttered authoritatively out into the brown sea. Zündel was standing on the dock. He had explained to the crew, with a believable show of fluster, that he wasn't actually a passenger but had just been seeing his wife to her cabin and had failed to hear the ship's horns, whereupon a couple of sailors had lowered a gangplank for his personal use.

See, I'm not so unworldly as all that. I can lie. I am competent.

Zündel stood on the dock and thought: perhaps my existence will change course? Maybe I would have drowned in Greece? Or fallen under a bus? Then again, perhaps I would have met the love of my life, either on the ferry or in the land of the Hellenes? My marriage would have been – Oh Lord – over, a new life would have begun. Whereas now, everything will remain as before.

There is something brusquely proprietorial in the way Zündel's tongue forces itself into the alien, still-soft gap in his gums. Curious, how a missing incisor can narrow one's perspectives. And how it can give one the sense of being the focal point of the whole world. He finds it almost incredible that he is not stared at by passersby, and if a friend were to tell him what Zündel is now busy telling himself, namely: the world has bigger problems, then he would reply: Asshole.

Oh, the hale individual can talk. But once his hair starts falling out, he won't care so much about hunger in the Third World. And when he has a festering carbuncle on his cheek, he will give it as much attention as he once gave the oppression of the working classes. What was it Albert said, who once claimed to Zündel that his social conscience forced him – rain or shine, in sickness or in health – to hand out flyers at least once a day? On Christmas Eve Albert had diverted his two little nephews by tying a rubber band round his nose, causing it to turn into a luminous red lump in the middle of his face. For five minutes, maybe, ten at the most. The following morning, Albert's nose was a blueish green hematoma. Albert spent the next fortnight at home and informed his comrades by telephone that he was undergoing a period of ideological reappraisal.

Ha.

But Zündel needs to eat. And then find himself a hotel. And sleep. Then see about tomorrow.

Du vin rouge ou blanc? asks the waiter, even though Zündel had ordered his meal in Italian. Blanc, he decrees, and is served red. The meat is gristly.

Has Zündel ever made a fuss in a restaurant? Complained about, much less rejected a corked bottle or an undercooked pork chop? Never once! Thirteen years ago in Sardinia – intimidated by the familial atmosphere in his pensione – he had eaten most of a sheep's cheese seething with little white maggots. It was the first time he had been made aware of the problems entailed by correct behavior, but other than that the episode had had no harmful consequences.

Waiters are poor saps. But hotel porters! They deserve to be torn into little pieces. They are masters of the black arts. Visit a city where a friend of yours has offered to put you up. Then late at night – as late as possible, to minimize your chances – turn up at a hotel, and ask for a room. You'll get it. You'll get it, even if the city is bursting at the seams with trade fairs. You'll get it because the fellow at the desk will be able to tell that you don't actually need his room. Now take the opposite case: you're shattered, exhausted, prepared to make any concession (upward and downward) in point of amenities. You just don't want to spend forever looking. You walk into the hotel. Are looked up and down. Sniffed. Rejected. Not because you're a dust-stained traveler, not because all the beds are full. No, because the man at the desk knows you're at his mercy.

Oddly, it didn't occur to Zündel till he had been turned away for the fifth time that it might be the gap in his teeth that made him look such a doubtful proposition. Of course. How wretched that must look, how seedy, how debile even.

At any rate, there seems to be little prospect of any milk of human kindness. So: to the station, the station.

At dawn, just outside Milano, a rumpled Zündel makes his way to the washroom. I am in motion, the train is in motion, the whole earth is in motion, and yet I lack all cheerfulness. Zündel tried whistling. On Sunday my sweetheart is taking me sailing. Zündel thought of his wife and the doctor, whom he pictured as featureless but stout. Magda had been a nurse, and Hartmut was her first proper boyfriend. He was a sailor, ergo the one who was taking her sailing.

The semi-circular sign on the WC read: Occupato. To indicate that there was someone waiting outside, Zündel tried the door anyway. It opened, and he had a shock. It was in fact unoccupied. But on the floor, between the toilet-bowl and the wall-mounted trash-receptacle, lay a finger. Zündel bent down disbelievingly to inspect it. It was a human finger, yellowish, encrusted with black blood, the nail blue. Straightaway, Zündel could sense he was not equal to this discovery. When he straightened up, he saw a wallet in the trash basket. He eyed it. Then he pulled out a cigarette, lit it, and thought: Keep cool, boy. – He pulled the wallet out of the wastepaper basket. It was his own, Zündel's, wallet.

Then the brakes squealed. Milano.

A dozen travelers were queuing in the Milan office of the railway police. Robbery victims off the night train. Handbags, wallets, attaché cases. Nothing about any finger, though. The women were gossiping away, the men looked aggrieved. Almost all of them were foreign tourists, Germans and Swiss. Zündel waited his turn. The man who was being attended to repeatedly called out his personals to the official: Hummelbauer Detlev, from Tauberbischofsheim. – The official had trouble with the details. – Umalbao? he asked uncertainly. – No, Hummelbauer, for Christ's sake! the German shouted back. Thieving bunch of illiterates! – The official failed to understand him, but still Zündel trembled. He was on the point of appealing to Herr Hummelbauer to pull himself together (was he really?) when one of the Swiss said to his wife: Did you hear that, Emmi? Good for him, I say. There's a man who refuses to be given the runaround!

Quickly, Zündel left the transport police office. He thought if he lacked the gumption to rebuke these fat and irate travelers, then he had no business reporting the theft of his two thousand francs.

2.

Lucifers stay in shadow. Recorders remain pallid. The loud tie of the chronicler may meet with admiration, but it has no place in the chronicles.

If I – or to be a little more forthcoming, if I, Viktor Busch – have chosen this moment to step forward, then it's only to reply to those fashionably skeptical individuals who take it upon themselves to ask who here is giving out information about Zündel: let me say then that I know Zündel's notebooks, I know Zündel's verbal protocols, and I know (or rather: knew) Konrad Zündel well – with all the usual limits that are conventional and perhaps applicable when it comes to claiming "knowledge" of another human being. I liked him. At the same time, I am not (was not) in thrall to him any more than he was to himself. Quite the opposite. All too often my view of Konrad's life was and is the same as his own: namely that of the habitual spectator and commentator.

Regardless of how well acquainted I am with the source materials, I feel no inclination to provide attributions for every last detail: this was in Zündel's notes, this was something he told me personally, this is something I heard from others, this is purely conjectural. If I had felt any such obligation to pedantry, then I would hardly have had the courage to tackle my friend.

A further word on the aforementioned "Notes." I was aware that he wrote, and it was palpable that he was ashamed of the fact. Once, I ventured to ask him what he was writing. Konrad said (and here, for instance, it is the gist of his reply I am giving, not his actual words): Oh, nothing, nothing, just for myself, so to speak therapeutic. – And after a while he said abruptly: You know, all those secret writers, with their desk drawers full of yellow pads, schoolteachers in the main (but other professions too), those writers-on-the-side, who exceed the median by that one hair's breadth that you need to be aware of your own mediocrity and suffer from it – isn't it disgusting and pathetic!

Ten weeks after Konrad's – what to call it?! – disappearance, I received a parcel from Canada. It contained a piece of plaster cast.

On a piece of card slipped in with it, I read – scrawled, no date – this odd sentence: For Pastor Busch, on the instructions of my apparently hopelessly lost son Konrad (see *verso*), the herewith enclosed. (signed) Hans Fischer, Vancouver. – P.S. Documents will follow under separate cover.

And on the back (in Konrad's equally scrawled hand):
Father! You never clapped eyes on me. You got Johanna pregnant that time in Genoa. Then you headed back north. Didn't know I had gray eyes, didn't know the least thing about me. Take this plaster cast, take these few sheets, they're a scanty lead to your son. Later, send everything to Pastor Busch in the horrible city of Zürich, he lives at 12 Birkenstrasse, and was kind to me. Must go now, cross my name off any lists and files.
In great haste, Konrad.

3.

So it was Monday morning, Zündel still had his passport and his change purse with some money and his train ticket, and he decided to go home and get his tooth seen to on Tuesday, and he stood in the phone box and he said to his Magda: So how was the bioenergetic weekend? –Where are you? asked Magda. – Something's cropped up, said Zündel, and felt revolting. – What happened, why aren't you on the ship? asked Magda. – I'm in Milan, but you're not being very nice to me, what's the matter? – I was asleep, said Magda. – What time is it? he asked. She said: Nine o'clock. – I'm sorry, said Zündel, I just wanted to let you know that I'll be home tonight. – Tonight? asked Magda unenthusiastically. – Yes, he persisted. – Koni, aren't you well? – I'll tell you everything when I see you, he said, appeased.

In the station buffet, he felt sick. The phone call had sapped him. – Increasingly everything in me curls up when I hear myself speak. I'm tired. Was Magda alone? All this continual assertion of self. Everything is hostile, everything that happens to me exceeds my capacity to endure it. Why does God have to send me a finger? And take my tooth. Sooner or later, everyone feels unviable. Humanity is assembled from partially reformed bed-wetters who never quite shake the feeling of existential displacement. No sphincter, no melancholy. Look at them, sipping their coffee.

He had bought himself a German newspaper for the journey, and was looking forward to reading it. But then the term "parcel of measures" kept him enraged almost as far as Como. On the other side of the border, he struggled for a long time with the notion of a saddle "with non-slip grip." There too, Zündel saw an imposing counter-position to his habitual slither through life.

He dozed as far as Göschenen.

Then he read an article about intestinal parasites. Belatedly, he found an explanation for the itching that had tormented him at night in bed, as a child. The female worms like to creep out a little at night, and lay their eggs just beyond the portals.

In Arth Guldau a young woman joined the train. Thus far Zündel had had the compartment to himself. When the woman hoisted her bag onto the luggage rack, he saw that her jeans were called "Let's Go." His own, he knew, were called "Happy Life." It occurred to Zündel to ask: Miss, do you think our trousers might be related? – But she sat down and said: You can't move without getting chatted up. – Zündel felt a shiver go down his spine. Had he been thinking aloud? Was it that bad? – Ever since Altdorf, she explained, I have been pestered by two Italians, and so I've finally moved compartments. – I see, he said, and added: Yes, the world is full of booty-hunters. – The expression, which had been one of Zündel's grandfather's, seemed unfamiliar to her, at any rate she looked at him uncomprehendingly, and immersed herself in her magazine.

Zündel's sympathies were with the two ill-bred Italians. He had long since observed that, under her very thin blouse, the woman was not wearing a bra. Now I don't mind seeing such things, in fact I probably rather like it, he thought, but in a way I hate it as well, and if I had power, I might well decree an end to immodesty. Everything is under protection nowadays, everything except for men. As if we didn't have to pull ourselves together, master ourselves, control ourselves enough as it was! And now these summer girls show up, and take feats of masculine self-mastery for granted. – I would like time to think this all over thoroughly, Zündel thought, and looked out of the window till Zürich, feeling increasingly irked by the frantic salubriousness of the Swiss scene.

The city looks as though a million tongues are continually licking it clean. The people dress smartly, although some few affect a kind of casual chic. Their dialect is broad, their gait is bent and cramped, and I'm an old curmudgeon, now here's my tram.

4.

In the stairwell, Zündel rather belatedly began to prepare for the reunion with Magda. Palpitations after five years of married life – I defy anyone else to do that. A gratin of leeks would do me fine, I'd be a bit disappointed if it was canned ravioli. Funny, ringing my own doorbell. Technically speaking, humiliating. Especially with no one answering. She's bound to be in the shower, where've I got my key?

Dear Konrad, I forgot to tell you I've got my women's group tonight. Don't wait up. Sleep tight. M.

Armed with his note, Zündel stalked through the flat. No little platter put out for him anywhere. Just the lime green plastic dish on the kitchen floor had a few lumps of catfood in it. – A year ago, I would have felt sorry for myself in this situation, but I've toughened up now, he thought, fighting back tears.

He ate a pear.

Later, he lay in the bathtub, not singing. He spoke: Ladies and gentlemen, singing in the bath is a cliché. Then he eyed the geyser and said in Magda's intonation: You know what, Koni, I think the liberation of women will be a good thing for you men as well! – Here's how! exclaimed Zündel, and let slip a resounding fart.

Before going to sleep, he bore a small missive into Magda's room and left it on her pillow: My dear wife, your accelerated development awes and impresses me! Sleep tight! Your K.

They had a late and surprisingly relaxed breakfast together, Konrad chatting about the blows of fate he had suffered, and since Magda was sympathetic, managing the occasional superior laugh. – My poor little man, she said. He unfurled his upper lip, and lisped: I like you very much, but I'm still going to bare my teeth at you. – Whereupon Magda said: I need to have a word with you, Konrad.

Magda: It was our decision – and we came to it jointly – that we would spend this summer apart. You said yourself it wasn't normal the way we've been cooped up together for years. Fine. You leave. And three days later, you're back again! And you leave a note on my pillow making fun of me. Have you any idea how aggressive that makes me feel? I'm no longer prepared to pay for my self-actualization in feelings of guilt toward you. I'm fed up with your touch on the hand-brake. And to be perfectly frank about it: the minute you left, I could feel myself flower, I could breathe again, there was fresh air.

Konrad: Your sentences have that *je ne sais quoi* of women's group about them. Your show of frankness is just as much "in" at the moment as your silly carrot trousers. At the same time, not one of those malcontent ladies is able to put a definition on self-actualization. It's nothing but gobbledygook! – Why don't we split up, I'll move out.

Magda: "Why don't we split up," that's all you ever say, that's your way of dodging conflict and silencing discussion.

Konrad: I impede your development, I poison your air, I choke you, I am responsible for your feelings of guilt – what is there to discuss? It's an open and shut case. It's an open and shut case, even though I'd be grateful for one single concrete instance, because I don't actually know what you're talking about.

Magda: You always have something against me. Ever since we've known each other, you've found fault with me! All the self-confidence I've lost in those years, because everything about me seems to irritate you. Surely you can't mean me to be afraid of you.

Konrad: Bloody hell, now what if you came out with one single example! What irritates me about you? What the fuck is meant to be irritating me so much?

Magda: Well, these trousers, to begin with.

Konrad: All right, *touché*. But god knows they're hardly essential.

Magda: Just a moment ago, after you got up, you came into the bathroom and asked me with barely concealed annoyance: Why do you always make that funny sound when you gargle?

Konrad: I've got a point, too. Your gargling is bizarre. Twice a day it makes my hair stand on end.

Magda: See.

Konrad: I was just having a laugh. Couldn't you tell?

Magda: No no no. I should hate you.

Etc.

Before long, they felt so desperate and cold and rejected that they went to bed together. And it was as though their bodies took no notice of the difficulties upstairs. Their flesh was still willing, still had the strength to overrule their dissident brains.

Half past three found Zündel in the dentist's waiting room, gripped by the weekly horoscope he found in one of the magazines. Each rubric, Life, Love, and Personal Finances offered a significant message for him. Sometimes you just need to give your heart a little push, it said under "Love." And the sector "Life" called for action as well: "Correct a certain error right away!" – He felt so profoundly addressed by this little astrological finger-wagging that he decided to act on it.

Just before five, Zündel was instructed to rinse for the last time. The freshly cemented tooth was merely temporary; the permanent replacement, which would be a perfect fit in form and color, needed to be made specially, and that would take a few weeks. But even the aesthetically less-than-perfect stand-in would, the dentist assured him, allow him to go on living and eating perfectly safely until further notice.

A chipper Zündel left the practice. And since he felt pretty much on top of things, he decided to stop off at his local.

At the usual table, as expected, he ran into some of the gang, whose effusive greetings moved him. Two of the women hugged him so hard he felt a little dizzy, though he well understood the premium on physical contact. – The talk happened to be of literature, and Zündel ordered: Don't mind me, carry on!

He heard: the new inwardness is just the traditional shopping and fucking squared. – Exactly. And so much odious solipsism finally makes you yawn. – Absolutely, you have to hand it to the old guard, they still have a sense of social engagement, our egocentric youngsters could learn a thing or two from them. – Believe me, in another two or three years no one will want to hear about Gen X anymore and those navel gazers will be washed up.

Zündel took advantage of the laughter to make good his disappearance. He felt relieved not to have been asked what he thought. – I know I suffer from muscular tension in my neck, he thought, but is it really any more than bracing against a perceived threat? Strange scene at the pub just now. More and more people strike me as unnatural and pretentious, but at the same time the disinhibited ones arouse my suspicion. And I keep meeting more and more principled characters, shrill creatures. But the undogmatic ratfinks aren't my cup of tea either. – Well, time to go home. Scary thought.

At home, he remembered something a painter friend of his had said: We have an ideal set up, my wife and I, we only communicate in writing. – Magda was out. Only this time there wasn't just a scrap of paper on the table waiting for him, but two full sheets of A4.

First sheet:

Dear K. I'm going to Bern for a few days to stay with Helen. Distance at the moment is more useful than these titanic rows. – In case you should have any plans to go anywhere yourself, please let me know. – I've just sat down again and made a list of all the things you have against me. It's a kind of postscript to our argument of this morning. The "concrete examples" you asked for, remember. – Ciao, look after yourself. Magda.

Second sheet:

Things you don't like about me:

That I turn on the hot water tap unnecessarily vigorously, that I tip the Nescafé out of the jar into my cup instead of using a spoon, that I squeeze the top of the toothpaste tube, and never fold up the bottom, that I am sometimes rough when I wind the clock, that I use too many fashionable expressions, that when pouring wine I forget to hold the bottle over the label, that I fail to put LPs back in the correct place after listening to them, that I leave the light on in the bathroom, that I always slouch around in jeans, and hardly ever put on a nice skirt, that I have an aggressive telephone manner, that I'm like two different people when we're in company and by ourselves, that I henna my hair, that I tend to give up novels half way through, that instead of a proper purse, I carry my change around in a ropy old tin can, that I put the stress on the wrong syllable with some words, that my M's aren't like the rest of my handwriting, that I walk around the kitchen in bare feet and then complain about getting a sore throat, that I scrape butter off the top of a pat with my knife, instead of cutting off a little bit at the side, that . . .

Zündel sat impassively at the table. After a few seconds he unleashed such a piercing yell that the cat leaped up and shook itself: Goddamned bloody women!

Time for another bath. Bath and bed, he thought, everything else is hyperborean. Teeth-chattering glacial moraine of a world. Still, better an icicle than a warmth-craving eejit. Subzero is the battle-cry! No to the womb. No to the man craving the return thereto. Long live the deep freeze! Long live the steel filing cabinet!

Eventually a man has to grow up, Herr Zündel, isn't that right, show a little maturity, a little toughness, everyone knows that baths are for babies. It's time to get real, Herr Zündel, and in real life people take cold showers: that steels, toughens, makes a man of you. All the whiners, Herr Zündel, all the sissies and softies, the humanists, the pacifists, the utopians, the idealists, in short, that mawkish minority that has never managed to free itself from bed and bath, they're always rabbiting on about warmth and protection, and any sober citizen, Herr Zündel, will recognize these wimps a mile away by their floppy attitude.

Zündel added more hot water and replied: Mr. Mature Gentleman, sir, I am sorry I am still talking to the likes of you. I am now over thirty and I still lack the decency to break off all contact with you and the likes of you, you nameless monstrous specimens. Cool and steely, martial and self-opinionated, upright and manly, you trample into the dirt whatever doesn't worship at your cult of death, you mummies, you caterpillar tracks, you polar miseries. Verily I say unto you: Something sensitive will make its way through this life sooner than anything brutish will get into Heaven.

Perhaps I was exaggerating, thought Zündel, as he pulled out the plug. Neither will anything sensitive get through life, nor will anything brutish fail to make it to heaven. The heavenly hosts that surround Our Father are after all hosts, and that doesn't sound sensitive to me. And basically no one can be too upset with the fact that He prefers the enthusiasts who admire His creation, seeing it as an adventure playground for pachyderms, with promotion beckoning for outstanding valor. Or is Our Father supposed to admit those trials who all their lives complain about His Cosmos, and berate Him? Is Heaven a fit place for broken-backed whingers? Are wing-weary melancholiacs suitable angel material? Is there not a place for them all where their craving for warmth can be satisfied and more – a place of a thousand flickering fires?

When Zündel climbed out of the bath, he thought: I don't understand much, but I'd like not to understand anything at all. I'd like to wake up one day and feel: all right, this is it, as of today, we're going to have no more intellection. The end of approbation. The end of condemnation. I want to be able to sit on a park bench and say: You know, I really couldn't care less.

5.

That same evening, about half past nine, the phone rang in our flat. Vroni picked it up, and passed it to me with the whisper: For you, Viktor, it's Konrad.

Supposing Zündel to be long gone and far away, I was surprised to hear from him. He said: I can tell I'm disturbing you, and I'm sorry, the telephone is a chancy tool. – I'm glad to hear from you, Konrad, you're not bothering me at all. – One is always a nuisance, he replied, a nuisance from birth. – I said: That's such a contentious statement that I'd like to have it out with you right away, are you at home? – Yes, he said, but I expect you were just going to bed, you don't have holidays after all. (Striking technique of Konrad's: he would always anticipate possible rejection by offering you arguments that made rejection justifiable, understandable, all but inevitable.) – I tried to placate him: You know I rarely go to bed before midnight. – He: If someone . . . – Zündel paused. I said: If someone? – He: If someone . . . I'm just thinking aloud, but isn't it like this: if someone says he wants to see me, if he's prepared to meet me, then theoretically there are three . . . – Once again Konrad stalled, and I asked: Three what? – Oh, crap, he said, it's not true anyway, all right, listen, can I pop up and see you for a minute?

It was eleven o'clock before Zündel showed up. On the landing he was saying: Incredible, the things that are done to us, but we stand for it! – Beer or wine? I asked, pushing him gently into the sitting room. – Something harder! he called out. Has Vroni gone to bed already? – Yes, she says hi, but she was feeling very tired. – I see, she says hi, he mumbled, I see, I'm always tired too, always

always tired, I'd like to sleep for a hundred thousand hours while the world turns. – Kirsch, whiskey or brandy? I asked. – Wine, he said.

Ah, Konrad, it's nice you're here, what shall we drink to? Love? – Oh, give over, he said, what a thing to say. – But didn't you once refer to it as a tropical island in the middle of a sea of ice? – I said that? he asked, really? Pure kitsch. Love is nothing but chronic anxiety punctuated by occasional spasms of pleasure. – Is anything the matter with Magda? I asked. – She's gone!

Later, after he had told the story (including that of his unscheduled early return), I asked him whether he meant everything he said, with his opening sentence out on the landing. – No, he said, that was a reference to a sign he'd seen on the tram – thousands of people must see it every day, read it and stand for it, and even for me it was the first time I hoisted in that bestiality – well, what it says is: Exit promptly – doors close automatically! – Zündel looked at me expectantly. I looked back at him. Finally, he said: Well, I was just thinking that it wasn't every day that you get such a perfect coincidence of actual and metaphorical contempt.

One day, he went on, he meant to write a pamphlet that would skewer the fear-mongers and suffering-merchants, a kind of compendium of contemporary skullduggery, a reaching out to the silent and the discouraged, who shuffled around in a daze, with outbreaks of panic sweat each time one of those wolves asked them what they were after. – Wolves? I asked. – That's right, he said, and pulled out a piece of paper: I thought this might make a beginning for my screed, I wrote it earlier this evening.

One day the hungry wolf asked the sheep about the nature of its objections to the world as presently constituted. – May I be perfectly open with you? asked the sheep. – Of course! replied the wolf. – Well, said the sheep nervously, everything in this vale of tears feels just a tad wolfish to me. – I see! replied the wolf, baring his fangs. But if that's enough to make you blub, how do you think you'll survive a proper mauling?

What do you think? asked Zündel tensely. – I see, I replied. – Do you think it's stupid? he asked. – I said: Why don't you ask me if I like it? – He thought for a while, took a sip of wine, lit a cigarette, and said: To make it easier for you to reply, to guard against direct answers, and to elicit from you the desired "No, it's not at all stupid." A categorical positive I wouldn't believe, a categorical negative I couldn't endure. By the way, Viktor, I've got a question for you: I expect you have some sense of how often you and Vroni have sex; would you be able to say how often you upbraid her for something, how often – say in a year, on average – you criticize her, tell her off, rebuke her? – What on earth has that got to do with your fable? I asked him. – There is some indirect connection, but first I need you to answer. – I've never thought about it, I said, perhaps I should attend to it a bit more, but at a rough estimate, maybe twice if you count criticism out of concern, as for instance: Must you sit in the draft? – Twice a year? Konrad looked up at me. – No, twice a week of course, I corrected him. – He asked me for my pocket calculator.

OK, he said after a few minutes, you got married five years ago, same time as we did, and it seems that in the period of your marriage you've leveled some 570 criticisms at Vroni! And me? Magda was barely able to scrape together twenty little reproaches – she wrote them all down for me, that's something I didn't mention to you previously – twenty criticisms in five years, that makes four per annum, 0.07 in a week and 0.01 per day. Imagine! One hundredth of a criticism per day is enough to kill off your marriage, and so on and so forth, I'm sorry, I'm talking you to death, I'd better go home. – But you still owe me a reply, I said, on the matter of the wolf and the sheep. – To which Zündel (more or less): Every atmospheric low in the so-called intimate or personal sphere heightens my sensitivity to foulness. The general air may be, objectively speaking, sullied, but it's only as a private casualty that I sniff the ordure. And so it comes about that instead of meditating on the particular, here, the crisis in my marriage, I allow myself to be distracted by the wider condition of the general. Hence the fable. And as I say, one day all wolves will be brought to account, pitilessly, only it will take many years for my sheep's claws to become sufficiently sharp and sufficiently terrifying in my doubtless fearsome paws. – Zündel laughed heartily, and I laughed with him, and we drank to his paws. Then he said: No, it's not on their account that the time is not yet ripe for retribution and counter-blow, but because the energy source for such an enterprise must not be hatred or private pain. Neither stand a chance against cunning and might. Something more positive needs to grow in me and give me sustenance, something luminous. Only if you argue from inner plenitude, from happiness, from love, only then will you come out victorious. – So long as, I said, so long as you still have any inclination to argue. – Ha, you're right, you rascal, and there I was, moved to tears by my own insight, which, in spite of all, I will cling on to.

Zündel stayed until four in the morning. He talked a lot of stuff. He avoided questions relating to Magda. He expressed himself vaguely about holiday plans. He spoke for a long time about his job, but when I asked him why he didn't give up teaching if it left him feeling so hollow and misshapen, he replied that having to answer questions was the opposite of contentment.

We stood outside the door, waiting for the taxi. Konrad drew in the early July morning air. I feel a bit sick, he said, but life's not all bad.

6.

Zündel was breakfasting, and noticing he was barely missing Magda. Peace and quiet at last, he remarked to the cat. At last I can sit over my coffee the way I like to. For years, I've been at pains not to belch. For years, I've held up my end of countless breakfast conversations, even though I'm naturally aphasic in the mornings. I was faithful, too, even though . . . well, just even though! A marriage is over when its "even thoughs" are not lived out, and if they are, it's over as well. So what do we conclude, Büsi dearest? Do you know that Magda had you snipped against my wishes? And now she just takes off, leaves us sitting there, and feels ever so bold. Mad! She needs to get her head examined. Well, see if we care. We're not the ones to force ourselves on anybody, and it would be a grave mistake to see Magda's presence as any sort of prerequisite for a happy existence.

Zündel took a headache tablet. It was eleven o'clock. He opened the window. The sun was out. I ought to get dressed, he thought, but I don't feel like it. One thinks he ought, the second doesn't feel like it, and the third has to decide one way or another. For the sake of simplicity all three are called Konrad. The intestine holds the sausage together. The name pretends it keeps us from disintegrating, but the compacted forcemeat remains flobby. The so-called I is only a foolish grammatical assertion, one that admittedly is increasingly brazen. The only reason we need our asylums is because not everyone likes to participate in this identity nonsense, and whoever doesn't fall for the planet-wide I-con is accounted mad. And now I'm going back to bed.

When Konrad breakfasted for the second time early in the evening, he felt worse. His sleep had been troubled and sweaty; when he got up, his muscles had grumblingly performed what he asked of them. His coffee cup shook in his hand, and the honey pot kept losing its definition. He thought he must have had nightmares, and remembered a falsetto voice that had kept dinning the same message into him. The only phrase he could remember was "dietary wagon."

He decided to give himself until midnight. Then he would have to make a decision as to how to proceed. What he was looking at initially was three and a half weeks of holiday, behind him lay a lifetime that had never, not for one hour, especially convinced him. His marriage – like the overwhelming majority of marriages – had probably been contracted through love, but this love turned out – like almost every other love (in his view) – to be a mixture of fear of solitude, sex drive, and habit. He had not taken up his profession out of pedagogical enthusiasm, but for want of alternatives, perhaps even because he had suffered so unspeakably during his own school days.

What now? he asked, after his bread and honey had been eaten up. In the first place, I'd like to get so far as to be able to see myself as negligible, as the little cosmic pea I really am. I want to be able to giggle about my existential earnestness and pampering of self. I'd like to be able to see myself retrospectively, as the banal prequel to a rotting corpse. And secondly, I wouldn't mind writing a little novel, were it not that so doing would reveal myself to be a self-important so-and-so, who – like any writer – has eyes only for himself, even in the strangest disguise.

Disquieted by the incompatibility of his desires, Zündel got out paper and pencil.

8.7. To write? (Perchance to publish?) If at least, one had the certainty of being a representative sort of cripple. What is at issue is not literary ability, but – putting it rather pompously – deservingness. To be worthy you have to be exceptional in some sort (for instance the cripple), but this exceptionalism must not be some random difference, it needs to be held up as a normal or compelling or statistically representative exceptionalism. (The writer can never be finally sure whether he's a crazy or an exemplary human being.) – Correction: the representative exception is extremely rare. Ordinarily, the representative is the common-or-garden varietal. An exemplary person would be the one who exposed the nullity of the average. If such a person were to write a book attacking his own average nullity, the result would be . . . oh, stuff it.

One thing for sure: whoever isn't prepared to get through life in discreet silence and without leaving his mark anywhere is a publicity-crazed scribbler. The end.

P.S. Though, in a more subtle way, the taciturn man is also making a fuss of himself.

Then Zündel remembered that he hadn't been down to the letterbox yet. The paper. The paper! It would help him get through the next hour or two.

He slid down the balustrade to the ground floor. On the bottom step, on a sheet of paper, lay a cigarette end. It had been ringed in green felt-tip. The ring was indicated by an arrow, emerging from another, speech-bubble-like form, in which the legend hovered: "Thank God decent tenants outnumber pigs like this." Schmocker the super's claim was rather flattering to those occupants who were not the delinquent. Zündel emptied his letterbox. In his ears he felt a sensation of heat that indicated to him he had little doubt as to his own culpability. Yes, of course, he was smoking in the taxi early this morning, then when he got home wondered what had become of the cigarette, and, panic-stricken, had scrabbled around on all fours looking for it. Of course. I'll have dropped it in the common parts, but Schmocker is and remains a dismal wretch.

Quickly, Zündel scuttled upstairs, but no sooner had he passed Schmocker's door than he heard the super's booming voice at his back: Evening, Herr Zündel! – Like a shot in the neck, thought Konrad, came to a dead stop, shuddered, turned, and forlornly boomed back: And a good evening to you too, Herr Schmocker. – Schmocker walked up to the bottom step. – So, we're on holiday again, are we? he bellowed from a range of six feet. – That's right, said Zündel. Schmocker raised his index finger, rotated it through 180 degrees so that it pointed straight down, and said: I know who was responsible for this outrage, you'll have seen it for yourself I'm sure. – Oh, who was it, then? asked Zündel. – Omarini, of course, who else! If it was up to me, I'd have had the building cleansed long ago, you take my meaning. – Actually, I don't, lied Zündel, to avoid excess complicity. – Eye-ties bish- bosh, bish-bosh! said Schmocker. – But there are some salubrious southerners too, replied Zündel, rather piano, and he wondered if he had ever said anything as pathetic in his life. Schmocker ignored him, and said: Has your brother-in-law left, then? – I don't understand. My brother-in-law? – Sure, your wife had her brother staying over the weekend. – Zündel paused a moment, then quickly smote himself across the brow with the rolled up newspaper: Oh, him, of course. Yes, he's left. – It couldn't have looked at all convincing. Schmocker made an indescribable face and yelled: Well, be seeing you, Herr Zündel, and remember, chin up! – What do you mean by that? asked Zündel. His voice didn't sound nearly innocent enough. And Schmocker answered under his breath, as though seeking some middle ground with Zündel's blurted question: Oh, just so. – And with that he turned, and disappeared back into his flat.

7.

How's it hanging, then, you little lustful brute? asked the hostess. Shocked, Zündel replied: Very well, thanks, and you? – She replied: No money, no love, just a basement full of filth. – And she grabbed him between the legs, and hissed into his ear: My name's Pussy, what's yours? – Oh, call me Traugott, said Zündel, paid, slid off his barstool, and wobbled home. Such exploits had never yet brought him relief. But at least the evening's yawning void was shortened by an hour.

Firstly, Magda has a sister but no brother, and secondly, Magda was away for the weekend at the bioenergetics seminar in Aarwangen.
That's the way it is then. No sooner am I gone than she brings someone home with her, they run into Schmocker on the stairs, and – for the sake of appearances – she claims the visitor is her brother. So shoddy. So conventional. The fellow was probably stretched out beside her, pinching her bottom, all the time I was talking to her from Milan. So it goes. And the minute I get home, a quarrel is manufactured to give her some legitimacy. Then off to Helen in Bern. Or should I say "Helen" in "Bern." Because his name won't be Helen. It's all such *vieux jeu*. Dear God, send me a hole to be sick in.
Zündel stood by the open window. The night was mild and bright. He stood and drank until – at about half past ten – he had the courage to call Helen's number. No reply.
What yesterday still had the appearance of value is sudden trash. Everything is subject to continual revision: so fragile is the past, so idiotically menaced by the least bit of now. A single

infidelity, and everything is swept away, certainly all the good bits. And the better it was, the more doubtful it becomes, in the light of one's doubts. In a matter of seconds, the love story is a crumpled tissue of lies. And if it weren't for the house rules, one might have a bath, because one's teeth are chattering, and existence is so unappetizing.

He turns on the radio and catches the end of an interview. A writer is saying: Over the course of time, I've felt the classics becoming like brothers to me. – Then the brother to the classics says: At the end of all dialectic is praise. – Zündel rediscovers sarcasm and thinks: so true, so beautiful, so bold. – At the same time, though, he can feel his eyes moisten. He shakes his head, and says, aloud: Konrad, Konrad.

He drinks calvados. He finds: for decades the course of events has borne me out. But this congruence leaves me neither proud nor happy. I wish I had a revolver.

Zündel drinks, smokes, flicks through one of the women's magazines lying on the coffee table, but midnight won't come. A reader's letter: I have yet to give myself to my lover, but I fear it may one day come to that. What should I do? The advice columnist replies: What you are so painfully and representatively going through is the crisis in orientation of the modern-day woman. Question your needs and work on your understanding of your emotions . . . – Oh, Jesus H. Christ, mutters Zündel, and stops reading.

The fact that Magda always laid the breakfast table before going to bed had always been a source of irritation to Konrad. The blithe, bossy manner with which the future's hash was settled in these parts alienated him, and he found it stultifyingly bourgeois to pretend there was no chance of an overnight catastrophe. Now, though, he lays out plate, cup, egg-cup, knife, and spoon, and at the top end of the table a tense little arrangement comes into being.

He casts an eye over the bookshelves. You wiseacres, you sages, you dolled-up yarn artists. There you are, united in the belief that you could shovel yourselves free with words. How long I put my money on you, how long I let you nest in the hollow spaces of my inexperience. But there's an end to all that now. Radical renunciation of the power of the mind, claiming to make sense of the world for me. You've turned me into a quote hamster. Your chitchat's at the root of my trouble. I want my feeling raw, not spoon-sized, I want action, not the book. I hereby declare – until further notice – that unfiltered reality is my aim, and I mean it. The mind – and I say it with all respect, and I have proof – the mind chokes off pleasure in living. The fact that the female praying mantis (*mantis religiosa*) bites the head off the male at the onset of copulation and thereby heightens his sexual prowess (the head contains inhibitor nerve centers) can surely come as no surprise. The spontaneous life is – headless.

Zündel empties the ashtray, airs the room, cleans his teeth, washes his face, locks the front door, gets undressed, and sits up in bed. Behind the alarm clock he encounters one of Magda's hair clips, picks it up, and sniffs it. A bland scent, he thinks, undecided between mournfulness and fury.

But in fact he feels strangely comforted. The Lord giveth, he whispers to himself several times. A conciliatory image floats into his mind: the Union of Abandoned Husbands (UAH) amalgamates with the Sisterhood of Beaten Wives (SBW). All hearts are thawed, the respective members exchange violets and melting looks, and body fearlessly presses against body.

With a sigh, Zündel turns the light off. He feels: there's a mechanism within us that degrades even the most shame-faced little idyll to utopian kitsch.

Then he turns the light on again and climbs out of bed. I forgot to lock the door, I must be getting senile. – He sees that the door is locked. Things are going downhill with me, he thinks, I've already locked the door. I really must be senile.

Midnight is past, in spite of his ultimatum to himself he has taken no decision, but what does another postponement matter? Isn't every lapse paid for by increased rigor?

Before he goes to sleep he remembers things they did for one another out of love at the beginning: in his single bed there were two pillows, one hard, one soft. When it looked as though Magda was going to stay the night with him for the very first time, he asked her which of the two she would like. – Which one do you want? she asked back. Although Konrad had a distinct preference for the hard one, he said he really didn't mind. Then Magda thought: he's bound to prefer the soft one, but doesn't trust himself to say so. I'll leave him that one, and take the hard one myself, though the soft one would be nicer for me. And so she said: I'd prefer the hard one. And he: And I prefer the soft one, isn't that convenient.

8.

Judith confirms he brought her the cat at nine o'clock on Thursday, and asked her tortuously if she would look after it until Magda, then in Bern, came home. He was going south. Since Konrad had looked very pale, and was unshaven and unkempt, she asked if there was anything she could do for him. He had replied that that was a creditable sentiment and thanked her for it, but he couldn't agree to anything right now, since he mustn't miss his train. To her question, whether Magda knew the cat was with her, Judith, he had replied: It's all written down.

In fact, when Magda came home on Saturday, she had no idea where the cat was, or where Zündel was. And furthermore – the information is given now, though it only came to light much later – Schmocker was lying. His account of the brother-in-law was pure malicious invention, and there was no possibility of a dubious visitor, much less lover, of Magda's, then or at any other time.

Information is reasonably plentiful about Zündel's stay in Genoa. However seedy and depressing the various hotels he selected – in accordance with his strange preferences (I myself have been to see them all since, at least once) – he did at least keep exhaustive notes on his thoughts and experiences at this time. The reasons that prompted him to go to Genoa, an inhospitable and rather gloomy working port, are at least partly clear: this is where he was sired thirty-three years previously, and this is also where he hoped to be able to acquire straightforwardly, and hence illegally, a handgun.

The notes of this week bespeak his isolation and a frightening rage at mankind. Interspersed with these are moments that betray an almost pathetic desire for love, a yearning for conciliation and harmony. And finally, almost ground up between the competing expressions of love and hate, is his commitment to a total apathy, without language and without compromise.

9.

On the southbound train Zündel shared a compartment for some
of the way with two senior officers in the Swiss Army. Because
he was so overtired, he had bought himself a first class ticket,
but there was no prospect of sleep now, the presence of the two
men was too distracting for that. They were so close to him he
could reach out and touch them, and yet miraculously they had
no authority over him! If he had been wearing his own military
uniform from national service, they would have ordered him out
of the compartment. Under the given circumstances, they had
asked him politely whether there happened to be two seats free,
and he had replied: Yes.

To begin with, they read. They tackled the local Zürich paper
together, and from time to time exchanged sections. Every so
often, one or other of them would shake his head. Zündel looked
up at the luggage rack and took in their caps: one major, one
lieutenant colonel. Officers' caps, he had felt from when he was
a child, led a mysterious life of their own. As did hats in general.
No other garment is so provocatively self-sufficient. For all that,
hats may sometimes make one curious about the wearer, but the
heads of his fellow travelers disappeared behind the pages of their
newspaper. Zündel tried to read them too, but from four feet
away, all he could decipher was the occasional headline. "Good
Digestion Essential to Well-being, Scientists Say." He was on the
point of evaluating this claim when the major lowered his part of
the paper, yawned, and said: Ah well. Whereupon the lieutenant
colonel also yawned, said: Ah well, and put down his part of the
paper.

Then both were silent, leaned back, and looked thoughtfully up at the ceiling ventilator.

Rover isn't what he used to be, said the lieutenant colonel at last. – Mine is fading too, replied the major, he'll be twelve in autumn, and yours? – A year older! But he's a good loyal fellow, a bit sluggish, his tumor is giving him trouble. – Any pain? asked the major. – The vet says not, but who's to know. – Quite so, quite so, said the major, and after a pause the lieutenant colonel said sorrowfully: He seems to be off his food though. – The major said: It's the same with Rex, but you know, he still enjoys his Tapsy. – The lieutenant colonel: Tapsy? Hang on, isn't that the firm that makes those chewing bones? A Swiss product, if I'm not mistaken. – You're right, said the major, but they're not what I have in mind, I'm referring to those air-dried fish flakes, I think they're from a Dutch firm rather than one of ours, but I'm not certain, in any case: he's quite devoted to them. – I see, said the lieutenant colonel, I'm not familiar with those. – Oodles of protein, said the major. Whereupon they both finally fell silent.

Zündel was frankly disappointed. He had been looking forward to a stimulating conversation on military leadership or national security. Instead of which, the two officers were talking about their dogs, and so giving each other proof of their humanity. Presumably they were more humane to their pets than their men, thought Zündel, and managed to rescue a little anger from the situation.

He betook himself to the dining car. The army, each time it hove into his consciousness, however innocently, had the effect of annoying him. It wasn't that he objected to national self-defense; at the most, he objected to its advocates.. The army was just alien to him. Just as there are people who dislike cut flowers or string music, so he had no use for the military. And over the course of time he noticed that men who did were not his cup of tea. But since he tended to get on with people even if they had a different set of preferences to himself, he concluded that a susceptibility for the military – as opposed to a liking for concrete poetry or liver sausage (neither of which was the case with Zündel, though he had friends who did) – that this susceptibility couldn't be a chance or secondary psychological factor, but was a direct representation of character. (It's a similar case – thus Zündel – with a person's voice: a loud, booming voice may not be disagreeable *per se*, but the association with its owner makes it so.)

In a word, Zündel's antipathy to soldiering was primarily his dislike to spending time with men who were enthusiastic soldiers, NCOs and officers.

His natural unease had been further exacerbated at recruit school: Zündel had the impression that most of the officers put national security at the service of their personal neuroses, and at best, vice versa. The pleasure in giving orders and taking charge; the appetite for uniformity and square-bashing; the fanaticism with which short back-and-sides, done-up collars and shiny mess-tins were insisted on – all these, to Zündel's mind, stood in no verifiable relation to love of country and national security. They had become autonomous compulsions and had lost all connection to any original purpose they might once have had. In fact, perversions was what they were. That was how Zündel saw it, who otherwise was at pains to be fair, even as his reservations over the course of time solidified into arguments that viewed what might once have been merely alien and irritating through the lenses of ethics and politics.

But almost always, when he got into arguments with supporters of the military, he would encounter a realism that was so unquestioningly robust, so shatteringly imperturbable that Zündel was apt to feel infantilized. His astonishment at the way people were unconditionally prepared to slaughter one another as soon as a few spiritually bereft father figures appeared on the scene, was probably a little naïve, and when he allowed the events of a day to pass review in bed at night, he no longer knew if the state of things that outraged him was an argument for the correctness of his position or – the said state of things – wasn't rather confirmation for those who had calmly decided to factor it, the state of things, into their calculations.

Zündel saw that there were many people who were inclined to deal with the available realities more or less trustingly. Their pliancy always paid off, since the existing state of things, broad-shouldered as it is, tends to offer shelter and confidence.

The realist is always right. As soon as he has buried the warmer ideals deeply enough, all he ever gets to hear is confirmation. When a war breaks out, he nods, flattered. Didn't he always say so? The catastrophe bore him out, and that was the pleasing side of it. The realist didn't ask for a war. That's why he was in favor of arms and armaments. But even the realist cannot avoid the inevitable, which is why he takes proper precautions. Then when it comes to pass, the inevitable, it merely proves how necessary the preparations were. The worst-case scenario is a fair judge. Whoever prepares for it never goes unrewarded.

When Zündel returned to the compartment, both officers were leaning deeply and crookedly back into the upholstery. Both were slumbering open-mouthed. Both were snoring, not loudly, but audibly. My God, thought Zündel, there I am in the dining-car racking my brains about national security, and those two are sawing away to themselves. He clambered over three legs, and resumed his seat.

I should like to be light-footed, he thought. Cheerful, balanced, and frivolous, a squirrel, my God, I can't manage it, I can't manage it.

And with that he too fell asleep.

Voices half-woke him, sounding like distant splashing, without meaning. Gradually he was able to pick out individual words, such as "Troop Concentrations" and "State of Readiness." Eventually, a whole sentence became snagged in his consciousness, and that finally woke him up: "The biggest pain in the bum are those men who shuffle past me instead of saluting me alertly and looking me in the eye."

Aha, thought Zündel, such are the preoccupations of these Rip Van Winkles, now things are getting interesting. He blinked his eyes, and was startled. The two gentlemen were upright, capped, and reaching for their briefcases. As the train started to brake, they left the compartment. They drew the sliding door shut gently after them. Zündel opened his eyes and saw that they had reached Bellinzona.

He thought of Zuberbühler. Zuberbühler was the association of choice not only for the army, but also for Bellinzona. It was there that that extraordinary pavour had put him under some pressure, the repetition course before last. One evening with drink taken.

Mate, he said, you're all right, but you're a hopeless intellectual. Zündel flew into a rage and replied: What's the difference between me and any other worker? I get tired at night. I get my biological drives at weekends. I belch, swear, fart, and drink beer. I do the lottery. I'm frustrated. What's supposed to be the big difference? – Zuberbühler had patted him on the back and said: But you're still an intellectual. – And Zündel, almost beseeching him: Why? – Zuberbühler, paternally: Because you don't know what you want. Because you're capable of endless suffering. Because you won't leave yourself or the world around you alone for just one second. Because the camera in your head whirs the whole time – even when you're fucking. That's why.

Gruffly, Zündel had said he knew what he wanted all right, but it couldn't be expressed that easily, the thing about fucking was something he, Zuberbühler, had no way of knowing, and reveille was at six.

During the hour-long wait between trains in Milano, Zündel sat in the station buffet again, on the same stool as four days before. Four days like four years. He thought of his grisly find. The finger had twice come up in his dreams. Waking too he took charge of the inexplicable, and wanted to wait for it to come clear.

There was a couple seated at the little table next to his. The young man was wearing a check shirt. He was sobbing silently. The woman stroked his neck, and dabbed away his tears with a piece of orange tissue-paper. How sweet, thought Zündel. North of here, women tend to get hard when men show weakness to them. Once, many years before, he thought he had been left by Magda, had sunk further and deeper into despair and hopelessness, had thirsted for just one tender word. At last Magda had sat down opposite him – upward of two feet – and said: We need to talk about our relationship. – And hadn't it been just like that this time, when he came home with his tooth gone, injured, oppressed, robbed? Oh yeah, I'm sitting somewhere, thinking about my wife, my profession, my handful of friends, I am dispensable to the nth degree, without much self-pity, without much future. The fact that I exist I can infer from the waiter, who gives me my change. – The meaning of life. You clear your throat when that comes into play, and you remember puberty. But the question of existence is sticky, and it's especially persistent in the case of those who – in the negative, of course – have long ago answered it. Odd, isn't it, that there are problems that have to be solved before they become pressing.

10.

In Genoa it was pouring with rain. He stood under the station arcades, looking up and across at the monument for Columbus, and thought: What am I doing here? What am I doing period. And where did he get his energy from? – I need to get my body to a hotel, or hope it will get me there. We're both exhausted. Come on then, it's getting dark, we'll find us a little place to lie down and wail at the rallying-cries of millennia.

Zündel took the first albergo he came to in the harbor quarter. The name of the albergo was just ALBERGO, or strictly speaking just ERGO, because the first three letters of the neon sign over the entrance gave no more illumination. The room itself: a dream of austerity. A bare neon ring hung down from the damp-stained ceiling. The walls, where plaster still adhered to them, were in a faded avocado green. The bed was iron, the chair plastic, wobbly and also light green. The wardrobe, whose door hung open, seeing as it had no lock and no key, had been given a lick of pale green paint. Under the washstand was a small yellow plastic bucket. No pictures on the walls. Not so much as a Virgin Mary.

Zündel tried to wash. The thread on the hot faucet was broken, and when he turned on the cold, it just produced an empty gurgle, then, just as he was on the point of giving up, a tiny trickle of water. – Always the same, he thought. Just as with women. They turn away, and when the man is half dead, they give him a little finger, and lo and behold the donkey, trembling with gratitude, sucks on it.

So he washed roughly. He noticed he kept thinking about Magda, and that he was feeling more and more miserable.

He lay down on the bed. Only now, with a shock, did he register the (apparent) loss of his wife, and feel how everything in him was connected to her, and that it was her love that had given him strength. And his pain only grew sharper when he sensed that there was no more fateful (if understandable) error than the elevation of the beloved into the unique provider of meaning in life. – Obviously, he was heartily familiar with this insight as a trivial theory, but worlds lay between what was merely known and what was abruptly and physically felt!

It is to be assumed that Zündel bit his stale pillow and tore his hair. That he was so bent by anguish that he could hardly breathe. That he appeared to himself as a squashed, godforsaken dung beetle. And it is to be assumed that his pain was not of the blissful sort that stays in one's head, not slipping down the gullet, thence to collect in heart and innards. – How foolish, insensitive, and inexperienced are those who would smile at suffering as self-pity, and reduce all grief to a masochistic pleasure.

I would like to say: that night something broke in Zündel. – But Vroni, my wife, is offended by the formulation, and thinks it sounds clichéd. Maybe so. I am a clergyman, in my line of work we do not despise formulaic expressions. Quite apart from which, I am writing for myself and for the silenced Konrad, not for a world that has forgotten benevolence, not for a world that is critical of certain turns of phrase, but continues to allow suffering. – Stet, therefore: in that first night in Genoa something must have broken in Zündel, just as a cracked and oft-repaired earthenware pot will eventually shatter.

Of course, the metaphor of the pot is hardly original, and it doesn't claim to give any information about the nature of what is broken. It only says that something frail, something damaged, one day broke. May I give it a name, Konrad? It was your trust, your always hesitant, always pessimistic faith in the dependability of man and the world. That night you were grabbed and shaken for the last time by the horror of birth. And your halting hope that, your cord cut and rejected as you were, you could still be made to feel at home, if only there were love, the love of one woman in particular, that hope broke in pieces. But could it ever keep what it promised? Did it not falter even at the stage of promise? Yes, it spread its arms wide – only to deliver a smack. (And the child turned pale, and choked and vomited forth its violet spew.)

Zündel woke early the next morning in an almost peaceful mood. The feeling of finally confirmed unbelonging seemed as it were stripped of fear and defiance. It was this feeling, this one bright and radiant certainty, that he meant to cling to. And if in future some mendacious you're-not-really-so-very-all-alone-as-that blandishment should approach him, be it ever so pleasing, then he would not allow one iota of his belief to be charmed away. The world – he thought, still a little crossly – the world has made me into an erratic block, well, let it bite its teeth out on me. Henceforth women and Easter bells and anything else that deceitfully rings and wheedles round me will smash.

He dawdled through his day, getting a little acquainted with the enormous Old Town. He drifted down lanes and byways. He relished the omnipresence of dirt. To him it was a sign of honesty, the way human squalor lay there unpackaged and stinking. The peeling doors stood open, failing to conceal further peeling stairwells and back courtyards. In fact, he was particularly keen on the facades of the buildings. They had no more pretensions. They were frank, baring with humility the gradations of their pastels decaying into wretchedness.

It smelled everywhere, and of all kinds of things. Zündel noted that he could identify the four cardinal points of frying oil, urine, fish, and excrement.

From time to time a plump whore on a stool in an entryway would pluck at his trouser-leg, herself also weathered. The cats were unbelievably scrawny. The main corso was crawling with people. Whoever was alone whistled to himself. All the others talked at the top of their voices. The tradesmen yelled, some tempting with popular tunes. – It came to his attention that all the stalls where pre-recorded cassettes were on sale also offered vibrators, and that the little tables of the black marketeers offered condoms as well as cigarettes.

Never had Zündel seen so many blatant pimps and crooks. They stood on every street corner, generally on one leg, the other bent back against the wall. They were on the lookout for johns or dupes for their fake gold watches, and they hissed "Hashish!" as Zündel gandered past.

It was with some relief that he registered the visible existence of an underworld. He thought of his planned purchase of a revolver and saw that his anxieties were groundless: the transaction would be successful, even straightforward. Even though there was no hurry, he already saw himself as a gun owner, and his heart beat joyfully.

Pippo Bar, July 10. The Colt in the drawer of the bedside table. Provisional MO: 1. Being able to leave at any time makes it easier to stay. 2. But no coquetry. 3. And no threats. 4. Get over any pleasurable fantasies of being mourned. 5. Withdraw from circulation in full knowledge of the world's immeasurable indifference. 6. Fleeting pangs of despair are not to count. 7. Not over a woman, please! 8. And all in all, motives of spite or revenge are unworthy. 9. Possible exceptions to be made for chronic melancholy and anything that powerfully, seriously, and lastingly draws one down. 10. And yet: if it can be arranged, try to choose as cheery a time as possible. Whoever leaves in tears or upset has chosen the wrong moment. 11. Keep in mind the banal truth: this kind of withdrawal is irreversible. 12. Consider too: relief (if you should be so lucky) comes to the living person, but not the corpse. End and relief are two separate things, even if you were brought up to think of them together. 13. Pass away calmly and with gratitude. Because: you have put it behind you. You were here, you were alive, albeit in your needy way, you put down your little roots.

Zündel went to bed early and tired. But he stayed awake for hours, vainly fighting off images of Magda's (supposed) unfaithfulness, vainly fighting off his hate which became increasingly immoderate. – Lubricious sow, he said, aloud. Low-down whore. Deceitful bitch. Shameless slut. Stupid, crude, lying, faithless, heartless, selfish cow.

He felt ashamed of himself, found himself alarmingly primitive. I don't really mean it that way, he whispered, and then he thought: Do I really not? What do we call someone who after years of intimacy and closeness gets rid of her companion just like that? Calls in evidence the involuntary nature of the emotions and gets the dust off her feet? Justifies herself moreover, by referring to her long-suppressed need to find herself? Doesn't scruple to invoke all at once everything that was bad about the relationship, and scrape together all the things that were inadequate about her partner? And how honest is the whole pompous ritual framing such a desertion, which in any case and invariably turns into a somersault straight into someone else's waiting arms? Why do people always say: "I turned to someone else for comfort because our relationship was rocky ..." Why don't they say: "I depend on your mistakes and the rotten things in our relationship, because they will be there to exculpate me and excuse my lack of faith ..." What are we going to call a creature that always pretends the ex post factum explanation or justification for their behavior was its motive and release?

Zündel pondered for a long time, rejected his previous terminology, and struggled through to the only just, albeit (in his eyes) somewhat pastoral-sounding reply: we will call such a creature not sow or cow, but human. Just human. Because that's the way we all are. In this central issue of the conduct of our lives there is dull conformity. Everyone is a more or less elegant, more or less resourceful escapologist, master of disguise and self-justifier, who knows how to lend dignity to his meanest steps. Every word is a coughed up bogie. Every sentence a slithery pretext. Skullduggery as a basic form of human existence. Dishonesty as second nature and principle of form. So we all lie and cheat our way from one falsehood to the next, from self-deception to self-deception, and in the end every death bed contains nothing but a stinking, slimy, loathsome bunch of deceit. – Forever and ever, amen, said Zündel, and soon after he fell asleep.

11.

For breakfast he drank a glass of grappa, followed by another one. – What will I do with this Saturday? he thought, and was pleased when he remembered his current theme was woman, and in a wider, more conciliatory sense, mankind. I could write up my nocturnal findings, and complete them during the course of the day. I could go from bar to bar, and reward myself with a little schnapps for each new thought. Maybe my conclusions will make a little vademecum? Surely no one would deny I had the necessary authority, in view of over three decades of bitter practical experience that would be absurd.

Zündel therefore decided to consecrate his Saturday to thinking and drinking. He knew of course that he wasn't drinking to reward himself for thinking, but because he wanted to drink and because he wasn't prepared to take full responsibility himself for what he was about to think (and to jot down).

He needed time to get the sleepless hours of the past night down on paper, and when he had done it to his own satisfaction, he ate a plate of spaghetti, drank half a liter of red, and napped until four.

And then he set off.

Tina Bar, July 11. The new dictionary. A handbook for myself and other latecomers. First part. – Nota bene: Egoism is now self-actualization. Consideration for others is loss of self. Brutality is truthfulness. Faithlessness is spontaneity. Lack of principle is openness to fresh experience. Hollowness is receptiveness. Inability to be alone is plays well with others.

Lola Bar, July 11. The new dictionary, part two. – Nota bene: Inconstancy is flexibility. Disinhibition is character. Thoughtlessness is impulsiveness. Availability for seduction is uncomplicatedness. Unreliability is autonomy. Superficiality is refreshing, disarming, healthy, uncomplicated naturalness, undistorted by excessive ratiocination.

Sereno Bar, July 11. The new dictionary, part three. Nota bene: Fear of the loss of the beloved is capitalistically infected ownership thinking. Fear of the loss of the beloved is bourgeois uptight jealousy. Fear of the loss of the beloved is squalid sexual envy. Fear of the loss of the beloved is infantile apron strings neurosis.

Stella Bar, July 11. *Liber Amoris.* Highly confidential. A memo for men. – Chapter 1: If you want to get rid of her, show her you need her. If you want to keep her, show her you want to lose her. – Chapter 2: If you are a friendly and devoted boyfriend or husband, then she will think: "He's sweet, he's terribly sweet, but Charlie – he makes me go weak at the knee!" If you treat her badly, she will think: "He's mean to me, but I love him so much!" – Chapter 3: If she says: "I do like Max!" then you can sleep easily at night. But if she says: "Oh him, he's got bandy legs!" then you have cause for concern. – Chapter 4: If she is unfaithful to you, it's your fault: you failed to satisfy her needs. If she is not unfaithful, it's your fault too: you kept her penned in. – Chapter 5: If you let her feel your trust, she will one day turn around and say: "Trust is only a subtle form of oppression." While if you say: "I don't trust you!" she will reply: "That's the wretched thing about our relationship." – Chapter 6: If you're jealous, she thinks: "He's constricting me." If you're not jealous, she says: "You don't love me anymore."

Balbi Bar, July 11. Continuation. – Chapter 7: She wants her independence. But also to remain Sleeping Beauty. – Chapter 8:

She wants to take the initiative. But she feels more at home in the role of victim. – Chapter 9: She craves tenderness. But she doesn't mind dreaming of something more uncomplicated. – Chapter 10: She wants security, she wants shelter. But not without an erotic component, not without an external fancy man.

Sayonara Bar, July 11. Appendix. – An example. From the animal kingdom. – Perhaps this is the most vivid demonstration of what we men are for and whence comes our melancholy. And it painfully shows us the way female creatures abuse God's creation. And demonstrates the deep ambivalence and inconsistency of so-called emancipation thinking. – Item. Last chapter (summary): the mosquito called *Johanseniella nitida* dances seductively around until an unsuspecting male takes fire, buzzes optimistically around her, and starts to copulate with her. She licks and nibbles away at him, and probably our hero is thinking: "Wow, this passion! I'm some fellow!" And then the seeming tendernesses turn into bites, she's hurting him, she's flaying him alive, she not only bites his head off, she eats him all up. But his penis is exempt. It sticks in her like a plug, the noble, saved penis, and lo, she keeps it and cherishes it.

Gramsci Bar, July 11, 8 P.M. – One-sided? Immature? Sweeping? Oh, kiss my ass! You moron. As if I didn't know there is no dirtier, cruder, more brutal, plain evil species on the planet than mankind. That every real calamity can be traced back to them, and that's the billionfold, verifiable truth! So much the worse, so much the worse! And so much the worse too for women, who won't shrink from the last and grisliest sin of all: they become agents of dastardy, and can think of nothing better than incessantly and complicitously rutting with these sons of darkness and profligacy. The end.

When Zündel drew a deep breath and put his notebook away, his neighbor at the bar gave him a friendly smile and said: Got trouble? – A little taken aback, Zündel replied: So-so. – Women? asked the stranger warmly. Zündel thought: an Austrian, but not an Austrian. And he replied evasively but not harshly, because he liked the man: There are other troubles too. – His neighbor nodded and said: But it's women that make the most trouble in this life, but they are so sweet and soft, and I like them. – Yes, of course, so do I, said Zündel, that's the bane of it, but tell me, where are you from?

The stranger was a Spaniard, grown up in Spain as the son of a Spanish father and an Austrian mother. Serafino was his name, and he did look somehow angelic to Zündel, in spite of his black hair. His complexion was pale and clear, his eyes (ultramarine) burned with an almost ecstatic glow. Konrad had never encountered a purer face. Pure, but not soft, at once somehow feminine and unarguably that of a man. And this so delicately put together fellow was a sailor, a seaman on a Libyan freighter which was sailing this very night – at two in the morning – for Tripoli.

Konrad and Serafino spent the evening together. They drank a lot, an awful lot, decidedly too much for Zündel, but what was born between them was more than an easy brotherhood. Deep affection conjoined them, a feeling of being related, of intimacy, as though they had known one another all their lives. They spoke little; the juke boxes in the bars they visited were too loud. Once Zündel asked: Do you think a man could get hold of a revolver here, I mean, without a permit? – Thereupon Serafino pulled him out into the alleyway and said: Of course. No problem. But it would be a waste! – What would? asked Zündel. – If you were to kill yourself! You'll see, life is short enough as it is. Are you unhappy? – Most of the time, said Zündel. Serafino squeezed his hand and said: Fratello mio.

They strolled along the port road, arm in arm. Zündel said: The woman I love has left me, but that wasn't what turned me against the world. – Serafino said after a while: The sad must not become extinct, otherwise Mary the comforter will die as well. – Zündel stopped and asked: Are you really a sailor?

The next bar they went to was called Krazy Korner, and seemed to be a meeting place for North Africans. Underworld! whispered Serafino. – Drugs? Zündel whispered back, and Serafino nodded. Zündel saw nothing suspicious, but then he didn't see much of anything anymore. He sensed that his next drink would be his last. He gripped the bar with both hands. – Help, everything's spinning, he thought, and at that moment the bar went quiet. – Police! whispered Serafino in Zündel's ear. A couple of carabinieri had taken up position outside the door. Zündel thought: I hope it's a raid with shooting, some action at last. – At the same time he noticed to his consternation that, as often happened when he had had a lot to drink, there was sudden strong pressure on his bladder. He hopped about on one leg then the other, and asked the barman urgently for the WC. – Non c'e, he was told. – Good God, groaned Zündel to Serafino, no toilet, what do I do now, I can't go another second. – Go out in the lane, but don't piss right in front of the cops, go round the corner! – Zündel sped out, and it is clear that the two bewildered carabinieri set off in hot pursuit. Of this Zündel, in his extremity, was unaware. He darted – already fiddling with his flies – along the lane, banked sharply round the corner, and after about ten yards on his left hand side saw an unlighted rear courtyard. What he didn't see was the chain, at thigh-level, that was drawn across the entrance. – His fall must have been terrible. Only: what was his pain in comparison to his humiliation, in comparison to his despair at the spontaneous passing of his water! In sodden trousers he knelt on the ground and vomited. And it was at this point that his two pursuers caught up to him. They lit the little bundle of misery with their flashlights and seemed to see right away that the fugitive was nothing but a drunk, who for reasons apparent had been in a hurry. Even so, they searched him, emptied his pockets, and checked his ID. – Aha, Svizzero, said one of them, while the other urged him in broken German: You go sleep now! – They helped him to his feet, and disappeared.

Zündel vomited again. After that he felt better.

When he limped back, pale-looking, into the Krazy Korner, barely half the clientele was still there. The rest had taken advantage of the distraction provided by Zündel, and scarpered.

My God, take a look at you! exclaimed Serafino. You're bleeding! And your clothes. Here! – Outside, he gave Zündel a quick hug and said: Povero, povero amico! – Zündel said: That's life, my life anyway, chains, falls, scrapes, and I'm afraid I pissed myself as well. I need to get out of these trousers.

Serafino waited in the Pippo Bar, next to Zündel's albergo. And Zündel washed, changed, examined himself in his pocket-mirror, and thought: I really am a poor devil!

He sniffed his trousers. For the first time in three decades, he thought of Rölfli Hunkeler, with whom he had gone to kindergarten for a year. Rölfli used to wet himself at half past ten every morning, and there was no force on earth that could get him to a toilet in time.

Konrad and Serafino drank an espresso together. Then they took a taxi to the harbor. They sat together on the back seat. Serafino held Zündel's hand, and squeezed it harder when the car stopped a long way out in front of a ghostly-looking freighter. – Goodbye! they both said at once. – I'll be back in a month or so, said Serafino. – I'll chop off my finger, said Zündel. – Why? asked Serafino. – I don't know, maybe to win the sympathy of the Virgin Mary. – Serafino said: Don't do that, she's with you anyway, and if you need me, just call, I have six wings.

Back in his room, Zündel vomited again. His little washbasin was half-full. He hoped it would drain away, got undressed, and went to bed. Everything hurt him. Everything spun as soon as he closed his eyes. In spite of which he thought: I must never forget there is beauty in the world, there is warmth in the world, there are good people and flowering trees. I want to be grateful for that, and cherish it. I must have always cherished it anyway, there is no other explanation for my hatred of ugliness. Perhaps the intensity of my opposition is proof of my tenderness. Yes, I'm sure that's right. Whoever doesn't violently reject evil can have no understanding of love. Goodnight, gray old Konrad.

If I'd been sober, I'd have broken my neck, he thought late on Sunday morning as he inspected his various abrasions, bruises, cuts and gashes. He could barely move. On top of that there was the alcohol throbbing mercilessly in his brain. He took a Saridon and dragged himself thirstily to the basin. – Not that as well! he thought, shuddering, because his vomit had failed to drain away. He had to empty it out by hand, scooping it into the same plastic bag as contained his underpants from yesterday. – What to make of the fact that almost everything that comes from within us smells bad, he thought. He dropped the plastic bag in the yellow plastic bin.

He got dressed. He packed his things, paid the bill, and moved across the way, to the Hotel Virginia.

12.

It's not an easy matter to reconstruct the following week. Probably Zündel didn't do much except write. But since he rarely dated his notes, it's hard to be certain what he put down when. One thing that is dated (July 14) is the description of the scene in the Ancona department store, the scene I set at the head of my account. – Also dated (July 15) is another entry that proves that Zündel knew about his father, even if he never shared his knowledge with anyone, not even Magda.

It goes, verbatim:

The man who sired me was, apparently, a sad dog, a man in human terms rich, a melancholy joker, brisk and dreamy, impulsive and charming, a sinful ascetic, a hermit with an appetite for love. Everything in him was inverted: heart on the right, liver and appendix on the left; he was a case of what the medical profession calls *Situs Inversus*. There's one such in every ten thousand, and it had to be my father, and I his son. – I inherited his pale gray eyes and his divided nature. – I never once saw him, and don't go by his name. (Just as he didn't go by his father's either.)

In 1919, at the age of eleven months, by the intercession of some international organization or other, he was brought across the Swiss border, as a mysterious collateral victim of the war. Made the lives of his adoptive parents, the Fischers, difficult. Was a gifted cuss and showed early signs of restlessness. Later on, he studied various subjects, got a girl pregnant, married her, joined his father-in-law's construction business, turned out, unexpectedly, to be extremely adept at it. Deepened his understanding of business. Fathered a second child. Enjoyed a secure existence.

On the eve of the day he was to take over the business, he walks into the kitchen. Says: Elisabeth, I've got everything I never wanted to have: a family, a business, a well-mapped future ahead of me. I can't breathe. Let's pack up and make a new beginning somewhere. – Elisabeth says sweetly: Don't make jokes like that, Hans.

Hans went off on his own.

People thought he was mad.

Six months later, Elisabeth gets a love-letter from her husband. He was in Alexandria, had found a job in a cotton exporting business, and was missing her and their children.

Already a little toughened, but still unsure what to do, Elisabeth takes advice from friends and family, and doesn't join him.

A few letters and official documents wing their way from Bern to Alexandria, and from Alexandria to Bern. The marriage is dissolved. For reasons unknown he remarries: a prostitute of Armenian extraction. For reasons again unknown, she leaves him before long.

Abruptly, in a profound depression, he leaves Egypt. Takes ship for Genoa. Arrives there in the middle of April '48 with a high fever. Is taken to hospital, and soon nursed back to health by Sister Johanna. She is young and warm and pretty, and best of all she's Swiss.

A never-experienced mutual passion. On May 2 they celebrate his thirtieth birthday and plight their troth one to another. On May 3 he says: I'm leaving tomorrow.

Johanna is incredulous.

Hans says: closeness is only possible through distance, physical presence kills passion. If we separate now, we'll hang on to each other. I love you, and can't imagine a life without you.

On May 4, Hans Fischer takes his exit. Destination unknown.

Johanna is wild with pain. She goes home to her parents. Spends day after day sitting in the garden in despair. Slits her wrists. Is found and put in an asylum. There, she suddenly feels something moving around inside her. From that point things start looking up.

In the icy January of 1949 she gave birth to me.

She never forgot him. Remained a spinster, never touched another man.

After four years, the first sign of life from him. From the north of Sweden. He had remained faithful to her. Would she join him? – She didn't have the strength to reply.

Three years later, she finally did manage a letter. She wrote: Today is our son's seventh birthday.

He responded right away, sent money, covered several pages, only the words "see" and "you" were missing.

Even so, the next summer she went to see him, unannounced.

To this day she hasn't told me what happened.

Now he's living in Canada, on his own, doesn't write often.

His script is like a flock of birds flying up in excitement.

His German is eccentric.

Maybe he was a cad.

I should like to see him one day.

13.

It wasn't till Saturday (July 18) that Konrad finally managed to write a few words to Magda. She didn't know where he was, and perhaps she was worried about him, who could say. He was still her husband, after all.

At the railway kiosk he bought a bland picture postcard (a blurred aerial photograph of the port) and wrote: Dear Magda, Judith is minding the cat, life here is good, no cross words and fried foods galore. Cheers, K.

He dropped the card in the red letterbox outside the railway post office. There, he thought, now I've reduced my wife to the rank of postcard addressee. She will think wistfully of the time I wrote her long letters.

He wandered round the station. He saw that everyone had some object in view. No one was going round in circles. With eerie determination everyone went on his way, heading somewhere, no question. It was as though they all had little purring motors strapped to their bottoms. – Isn't everything mysterious, Zündel said to himself, and made for a lavatory. While he looked down at his stream of urine, he thought: mind you don't lose contact with reality. Don't overdo the amazement. I've been away for a week, and already people are strange to me, and the most natural things startle me. So I think what I'll do now is buy myself a newspaper, there, after all I'm not an ostrich. I know there are more current things than me. I know too how much world history depends on our involvement. What's a boxing match without a public? A pallid dumbshow. What's a sermon without a congregation? A bit of absurd theater. What would politicians be without publicity? Masks of stiff cardboard or paper maché. Yes, but for us onlookers, world history would probably grind to a halt. We stir the doers to action and so give rise to a brisk and colorful pageant.

Zündel bought himself a Swiss paper, sat down at a little marble table, ordered a Campari, and no sooner had he begun reading with interest than he noticed his capacity to absorb information was reduced, that he kept getting stuck, that all these sentences and terms didn't bore him so much as simply disgust him.

Good in the air, credit rating, comfort zone. Jailbait. Humanitarian gesture. Organ-harvesting service. Plus pedophile community and re-insurance and arctic frontal system.

The swamp.

The Kremlin's stick-and-carrot policy and a generous offer from the White House and lockable paradises. The words stink and the sentences stink, as if they'd slipped out of the hemorrhoid-wreathed intestines of pest-infected morons. The stock market didn't get out of bed this morning, three-ply toilet paper is uncompromising, the intermediate missile program is on course. Shrill formulations are smeared over unresisting facts. Data spread their thighs and admit well-used linguistic particles. A noun acquires a stiff adjective and sticks it to reality from behind. Endless, shameless, comfortless sentences and contents pair off, and the product of their unchastity is called a newspaper.

At lunchtime, Zündel packed his swimming things and took a bus out to Nervi. The decision had taken a lot out of him, because the heat was extreme and he felt torpid. The more contentedly he now sat on an uncomfortably tilting slab of rock, slathered himself with sunblock, and thought: I am enjoying an active holiday. – A child's voice cried out: Mama, look, that man's all white! – A few yards behind Konrad was a deeply tanned family of Germans. The mother glanced at the pallid Zündel and said: Come on, Uschi, why don't you splash about a bit.

A family of Italians was just getting dressed. So cumbrously, you couldn't help looking. Mutual assistance was supposed to keep those parts from becoming public that in Italy were still the preserve of private life. – Prudish but well-intentioned, thought Zündel. Repressed, but more admirable than the grim topless honesty of cutting edge contemporary beaches.

The German Mama had followed her Uschi into the water. Papa was engrossed in the paper: "Yelling baby found in garbage pail."

Zündel had no words for that. He buried himself in his own reading matter, a paperback with the title "After the Big One: Adapting to Survival." Earthworms are very good for you because they are so protein-rich; he made a mental note of the fact. You drop them in boiling water. Then you slice them open with a knife, remove the grit, and wash them again, from the inside. Then grill them on a hot rock. Suggested vegetable accompaniment: tender young dandelion leaves.

Here was Mama and Uschi back again. Uschi had stepped on a sea urchin and was screaming. Papa said: Why don't you watch where you're going, you damned fool. – Don't be cross with her, it can happen to anyone, said Mama. Papa said: No, she could have kept her eyes open. – Then he went grumpily into the water.

Zündel made a mental note: never drink urine! Though in extreme emergencies (desert situation) you can make potable water from it: pee into a hole in the sand, and watch the poisonous liquid drain away. Place a container over the bottom of the hole and stretch a funnel shaped piece of PVC over the top of it. While the poisons remain in the ground, the liquid, drawn to the surface by the sun's heat, will condense against the taut plastic, and drip into the container.

The child was still crying.

The father came back from his swim. He was hobbling and shouting, I want to know who's in charge of this goddamned beach. I'm going to make a complaint. You wouldn't have a pair of tweezers would you, Mama? Sea urchin needles can easily turn septic. – I'm afraid not, honeybunch, they're back in the hotel, said Mama. Does it hurt very much?

Now Zündel took his turn in the sea, and in spite of the yellowish foam crests breaking around him, he enjoyed the cool water. Coming back on land he kept his eyes open, but still, as expected, stepped on a sea urchin.

On the way back to his spot, he disguised his limp for fear the German would involve him in a conversation about the laxness of the Italian authorities. But the German was now sitting between the legs of his wife, back to her, while she squeezed his zits. The long white worms of sebum were Zündel's cue to depart.

He arrived in his hotel salt-caked and sticky. Straightaway he stripped to his underpants, draped a towel across his shoulders and hurried out to the shower on the landing. Just outside it, he slowed his pace and almost reflexively pricked up his ears. From the shower room he heard a sound that was like the panting of a dog on a warm summer's day. He listened more closely: the sound was a duet. Great Scott, thought Zündel, and he hopped from one foot to the other, because he could see that the keyhole was generously proportioned. – What would the normal person do now, he wondered, probably beat a quick retreat, a little peek would be the act of a pervert. Shall I or shall I not? – The panting was loud and rhythmic, and now Zündel involuntarily bent down, squeezed his right eye shut, and applied his left to the keyhole. He saw a pink-tiled wall. Nothing else. – Just then the ghastly thing happened. Zündel received a violent kick up the behind that sent his forehead smashing against the door. For a split second there was complete silence, inside and out, but before Zündel, trembling with shock and humiliation, could stand upright, a high pitched voice began to scold him. It was the cleaning lady, identifiable by her bucket and mop. The man she had caught in the act stood stricken in front of her, staring down at her sandals. The couple in the shower room seemed to have been caught out as well, at any rate they weren't making any more noise. Maybe they were foreigners who hadn't understood the woman's Genoese dialect, and took the crashing and abuse upon themselves and what they had been doing. Either way, Zündel was only slowly able to part from the incensed female, and first slowly and then very quickly retired to his room. He locked the door, sat down dry mouthed on the bed, and thought that, in human terms, he was finished for the foreseeable future. He felt the bump on his brow. He remembered his beach reading. He groaned. Perhaps the hotel management was even now being informed of the monster on the second floor and his room number was being established?

Zündel waited.

No one knocked.

An hour later, he washed in the hand-basin.

He was hungry but didn't dare leave his room, and decided to skip supper.

He crawled under the sheet.

His head hurt, and his foot hurt.

How all alone I am, he thought, and he remembered the screaming baby in the garbage can.

Later he said to himself, very quickly, ten times in a row: organ harvesting.

A rough night. Bad dreams, toothache, thirst, and a blocked nose.

14.

Once again – that Friday aside – there followed a sequence of incident free days. Early on Sunday morning, Zündel left the Hotel Virginia and was now staying at the Albergo Armonia.

Blue ink: Zündel must have bought himself a pen; all the earlier records and some subsequent to the Genoese stay are in fine black felt-tip.

There is a further, almost alarming peculiarity in the Armonia protocols: at the end of one section – often a single sentence – Konrad would straightaway comment on what he had written with the expression, "load of crap." – Sometimes there seemed to be no form of words that did not elicit such a challenge, no statement that was allowed to stand.

A typical excerpt might run (verbatim):

Reality – with all equanimity, more terrible and indescribable by the day – forces one either to complete withdrawal or baying anarchy. –

I can neither steer the course of history toward some bearable ideal, nor can I deconstruct the ideal, to make history appear more tolerable by comparison. – Oh, load of crap.

The course of history commences at birth – Oh . . .

Get on the track of the emotions! (Cf. Zuberbühler: you don't know what you want!) Possible leads: Wife. Job. State of the world. Time the deceiver. Weather. Incisor. Bump on my brow. Rudeness met with. Apartment complex. Advertisement complex. The streetcar. A supermarket. People, people, the Schmockers, the politicians, imposing physiques, the whole object compulsion lobby, ruffians, shouters, bluffers, conmen, the wall-to-wall wolves.

Or maybe: the inheritance of my father. My mother's pregnancy. My birth in winter. Saturn? – Oh . . .
Dull-wittedness is an exact word, I like it. –
Negation is the only thing that keeps one alert, but strength, strength. – Survival training begins at birth. –
Giving up is cowardly. Carrying on is cowardly. Giving up is brave. Carrying on is brave. Life is a matter of vocabulary. – Ach, load of crap.

Out of who knows what state of feeling – it will hardly have been desire – Zündel, on Friday night, went with a prostitute for the first time in his life. She had accosted him on the street, and against his custom he had stopped and asked, half-shyly, half-masterfully, what she charged.

Then, shuffling along in her wake and thinking of what lay ahead, he began to feel afraid. He didn't feel like it. He couldn't do it, and after not quite fifty yards, he couldn't imagine anyone who could and would. – Why is this a flourishing profession? Are men just animals? Or machines? Or pathological impulsives who don't require affection and are in thrall to their fiery phallic wand?

By now they had crossed a gloomy courtyard, and it felt too late to Zündel to peel off. The woman who had kept turning round to him and flicking her tongue out in his direction – presumably thinking she was heightening his interest – now entered a long and dimly lit passage, at the end of which was a porter's lodge. Evidently a convenience hotel, thought Zündel following after, and at the same moment he saw with a shock where he was. The Armonia! He groaned inwardly, but the scrawny porter beamed all over his face for the first time, and called out in a voice of thunder: "Benvenuto Signor Sindel!" – Zündel broke into a cold sweat, managed a "buona sera," cursed his enterprise, his blindness, cursed all rear entrances everywhere and concluded he would be spared no humiliation.

He found himself going up a narrow spiral staircase, then left, then right, then into the woman's room.

She closed the door and demanded her money upfront. It was a little more than the sum agreed, but for that they would enjoy amore italiano. – Zündel wondered if amore italiano corresponded to the practice known to him as "French love." He hoped not, and paid. She stripped off her skirt and pants, went to the sink, and swabbed herself cursorily with a green sponge. Zündel looked about him. His eye caught on a yellow woven plastic wastebasket beside the bed, half full of used condoms. He shuddered. The woman stepped up to him and unzipped his trousers. She said mechanically: amore amore. Straightaway he pulled the zip up again. Then she lay down on the bed and parted her legs. She thrust her pelvis at him once or twice, and moaned noisily. He stepped up to the bedside and looked at her. The only natural thing about her, the only loveable thing was her ugliness, everything else about her struck him as dead. – You no like-a me? she asked, and grabbed for his flies again. He looked down at the innumerable blue veins in her thighs. – No, no, I do, he said, but I'm not in the mood. – She sat up and shrieked: What about the money? – You keep it, said Zündel, hurried out, and sadly betook himself to his own room.

15.

The last week of the vacation began. He was less and less able to explain why, once the dentist had given him his provisional tooth, he hadn't gone on to Greece as he'd originally planned. He was sitting out the loveliest days of July, or sleeping them away in stuffy pensiones, dawdling them away in lanes that seemed ever narrower, ever dingier.

His feeling of wretchedness on waking intensified by the day, so that he would often stay in bed till eleven, twelve or even two o'clock and wait till he felt better. The only effect of so much brooding and drowsing was to make his head and body feel even heavier. Then he would have the sensation of lying in a lukewarm pond, wreathed in creeping plants, impassively waiting for decomposition to set in.

He didn't think of Magda often. His attacks of aggressive pining for her became less frequent. His wife seemed almost as remote to him as the dog that had bitten him two years previously, in the course of a hike in the Bernese Oberland.

School felt equally remote. Classes were due to resume in under a week. Unimaginable. Unimaginable, the idea of speaking, having to speak in the teeth of his deep desire to remain silent. – Good morning, everyone, I hope you enjoyed your holidays. Right, as we're all fresh and well-rested and tanned, let's get cracking on the Thirty Years' War, shall we?

And to be sitting in the common room again, little conversations lapping all around him, little murmurs of news. His right ear picks up: A willing pupil, not exactly the sharpest tool in the box, but willing. – His left ear picks up: Stress is just a word. – His right picks up: I tell you, no one grills meat like the Yugoslavs. – His left hears: According to Duden, the dative is permissible.

Unimaginable.

And to be back in Schmocker's building! The daily gauntlet of the stairwell. The Lustenbergers' fixation with Brussels sprouts. Schmocker junior's nightly trumpet practice. Last thing at night: Magda laying the table for breakfast. Late edition of the news: homeopathic doses of the day's brutalities. Cleaning his teeth. One last flush, and to read for the ten thousandth time: your toilet seat is not screwed down but stuck on, in the interests of efficient cleaning.

Unimaginable.

16.

Portofino is world-renowned, and on Wednesday Zündel managed to get up at nine. – Today we're going on an excursion, old paleface, he said into the mirror. We're going to Portofino, what do you say. Nietzsche was there. And the restless spirit of some French writer found peace there too. So, avanti!

By train to Santa Margherita. Palms, orange groves, tourists. Onward journey by ferry or bus. Let's say ferry. Bus is everyday, ship is more festive.

Great crowds of people were milling around on the quay. Among them a tour group from Germany. What a language, thinks Zündel, and to amuse himself he makes up little equations: Italian to German is like angora hair to boar bristle. Or: Italian to German is like ballet shoes to clodhoppers, or cherry to garlic.

Here comes the ship, toots its horn, docks, and with voice cracking with intensity, the leader of the German tour group yells: All right everyone, occupy the top deck!

Zündel takes the bus.

So this is Portofino. Knickknack stalls, boutiques, yachts, jolly-boats and snap-happy tourists, but otherwise really very picturesque. There's even a fisherman repairing his net, a fellow worth taking a picture of with his sinewy sinews and chest hair.

Konrad has managed to find an empty table under a sunshade. He orders a cappuccino. The piazza is spread out in front of him like a bustling theater stage.

He smokes and looks round and feels good. For minutes on end, he admires the people. The women too. The women even especially. Especially the one woman who walks so harmoniously across the square, not so much walking as floating, and has now stopped, then floats on at an obtuse angle to her progress thus far, which is to say: making straight for Zündel.

O benevolence rewarded. O terror. She's joining me at my table. Puts her hand on my arm. Says simply: Bonjour, ça va? He gulps and says Oui. – She says: Tu es Suisse, n'est-ce pas? – He stammers Oui a second time. (No doubt she finds me dull as anything, and is bitterly regretting her impulse.) But she smiles at him and whispers: Tu me plais. – He can't even say Oui to that. Just sips in consternation at his cappuccino.

She says in German – she has the sweetest accent: I'm Nadine, no, I'm Eve – oh, tell you what, just call me Nounou! No one's ever called me Nounou!

Suddenly Konrad feels a little easier. He says: And I'm Traugott, but that's a bit hard for you to say, so why don't you just call me Pansoti. That's a type of Ligurian pasta that I'm especially fond of.

Nounou giggles and asks: Do you know what "Nounou" is? – No, says Zündel. – She says: Nounou is the name of a Greek brand of condensed milk that I'm especially partial to. – Are you Greek? he asks. – Part, she replies, but don't quiz me. Will you have supper with me? – Zündel, confused: Do you live here then? – Nounou repeats: Will you have supper with me? – He asks: When? – She says: Now, today, tonight! – He reflects and before he can say anything she gets up and says: Eh bien, then skip it. – Zündel quickly: Oh, yes, yes please! – Slowly and softly Nounou says: But not today! – And she leaves without saying goodbye.

He sits there, stunned. Sees a couple of puffy Swiss at the table beside him stare after his disappearing Nounou, hears one of them say: Not so bad! hears the other saying: But her legs could be longer! – and his bewilderment at Nounou's behavior gives way to fury about those thick-rumped fellows and indignation at the unquestioning alacrity with which the least attractive of men deliver themselves of aesthetic judgments on women.

They make ready to leave. They summon the waiter. They address him in a sort of German that German speakers believe is well-adapted to understanding by Italians. They say: Listen, you, not cheat us! – The waiter doesn't react and tells them what they owe. They think the price is outrageous, and complain. In the end, they pay. Finally they get up, and as they do, they secretly pocket their coffee spoons.

Zündel has seen them do it.

This time, he didn't keep quiet about it.

He said: Put those spoons back, or I'll make a fuss.

They gawped at him vacantly, then grinned like idiots, and quickly put the spoons back.

Good for you, Zündel! thought Zündel. A victory at last.

He drank a couple of almond liqueurs.

Then Nounou came back, took his face between her hands, and said: Bonjour, Pansoti! – He said nothing, but thought: You whimsical can of Greek condensed milk. – She looked at him inquiringly with her orange-brown eyes and whispered: On y va?

Her apartment in the historic center of Rapallo was dark and tiny. Nounou put on a scratched flamenco record and braided her black hair into a plait. Then she started cooking rice. Every so often she opened a jar of blueberry jam, dipped her middle finger into it, and licked it clean.

Zündel watched her from the little sitting room. He was sitting in a leather armchair like a boxing glove. On the floor in front of him were innumerable printed outlines, some still pristine, others already colored in, all with the same subject: little boats in a bay against a beach promenade with palm trees in front of a picturesque row of houses under a sky with cumulus clouds. – Good Lord! thought Zündel, and at the same moment Nounou called out: That's what I live off, tourists can't get enough of them! – He called back: Why is your German so good? – Nounou called: Leave me alone! – Do you mind if I smoke? he asked. She didn't say anything, but hopped into the sitting room on one leg and kissed Konrad on the mouth. Then she sat down cross-legged on the floor and stared into empty space for several minutes. Before she got up to check on her rice, she said: I'm not a great talker.

Her voice was dark and beautiful.

Zündel didn't eat much. He hadn't been hungry for days. But to settle his nerves, he helped himself to wine. – Alcohol helps me rise to the occasion, he said to Nounou. After five or six glasses the police dog in my brain loses most of its teeth. After two more it stops growling, and the present becomes frictionless and silky. Perhaps love of alcohol is the logical outcome of a culture that takes each minute of life as requiring commentary and control and justification. – Am I talking too much for you? – Nounou said: I had a girlfriend at school. She had three big boards up in her room. One over her bed, one over her desk, and one beside the door. On each one of these boards was the same slogan. On her twenty-first birthday she swallowed eighty painkillers. Her name was Beatrice.

Nounou fell silent, and Zündel asked impatiently what was written on the boards. – Guess! she said. He guessed: Always look on the bright side? – Wrong, absolutely wrong! – *Arbeit macht frei*? – No! – Remember to wash your hands? – Warmer! – God is watching? – Almost! said Nounou, but more psychological delicacy. – I give up! said Konrad. – Kiss me, and I'll tell you, she said. He leaned forward across the table, but before he had reached her lips, she had put out her hands, pushed him away and cried in horror: What would Jesus say? – For a moment, Zündel was so bewildered that Nounou squealed with delight. – Now you know! she said. Poor Beatrice. Jesus was her police dog.

After a while he said: Parents like that deserve a good whipping! – No! she exclaimed. – Yes! he shouted back. – No, she said, all parents deserve a good whipping, because they all get everything wrong. But since most people are grateful for their parents' mistakes, because those mistakes excuse their own, the parents don't deserve a good whipping. Voila. You probably want to go to bed with me now?

I'm not sure, he said. – But I am! declared Nounou. I know. You men all have sex on the brain. You'll spend all evening talking to a woman, but all your sentences have a lurking quality and your eyes betray a secret regret that these sentences, which only delay the moment of seizing us, are necessary at all.

Zündel said: There was once a little mother who had seven daughters. One day she called them all to her and said: My dear little daughters, beware of men, they only ever want one thing. They are terrible dissemblers, but they have a vulgar organ that always gives them away. – What organ is that? the little daughters asked. The little mother said: I have to go now, otherwise I'll miss my bus. – The good little daughters said: Dear Mama, we promise to be on our guard, today and always.

Haha, replied Nounou and stuck out her tongue at Zündel. Then she disappeared into the bedroom. A little later she was standing in front of him completely naked, saying: Je suis jolie, n'est-ce pas, Pansoti, je suis jolie! – But he didn't touch her and said: You're standing so near me I can't see you. – Nounou said: Je suis nue, mais toi aussi, Pansoti, tu es perdu! – You're so right, he said with feeling, you're so right.

Later they lay together side by side like brother and sister. Nounou said: I think I understand my husband now. He was always differently wired to me, in sexual, emotional terms. Do you want to hear? All right. My husband always felt like sleeping with me when we were alienated, when there were tensions, discords, disunities in our relationship that threw us both behind our personal frontiers. It was like having two bird cages in the room, each with a canary in it, furiously pecking and yearning at its grille. Right. In those sorts of situations, my husband liked to feel me – and I didn't. I liked to feel him when we were terribly close to each other emotionally, sort of as a physical seal to that closeness. But at those times he had no desire for me at all. Emotional harmony seemed to stop his drive, while it aroused mine. For him, sex was a means to overcome alienation, for me it's an expression of existing closeness. Voilà. We had to split up. Are you asleep? – No, said Zündel. – Am I a chatterbox? – No, he said, I like listening to you. – Do you want to tell me about yourself? – Not really, he replied. – She asked: Do you want me to blow out the candle? – Konrad said: So why is it you suddenly understand your husband now? – Because with you I feel the way he did with me. You are so strangely familiar to me and dear, that a violent contact would seem almost destructive, and certainly unnecessary. – Yes, sighed Zündel, physical desire is all well and good, but I never set much store by that breaching of frontiers either. Bodies smacking against each other remain strange, perhaps that's why the so-called sexual act feels so absurd and bloody-minded, and maybe that's why any reasonable person will feel a bit dismayed, even after the most apparently successful coition. Where is he now? – Who? asked Nounou. – Your husband. – He's dead, she said. Three months after we broke up, he fell in the Dolomites. He was Swiss like you. He even resembled you a bit. When I saw you sitting at your table all alone, I had a shock because you were so like Martin. – Zündel said: That's a little bit disappointing for me. – How come? she asked. – Because you didn't like me for my own sake, but on account of him. I'm just a stand-in. – But that's always how things are, you silly Pansoti, said Nounou, kissing

him on the eyes. Every couple is just a couple of stop-gaps! Love
is never anything but the mutual willingness to replace the other's
original. – You're mad, said Zündel, and Nounou replied sleepily:
Do you think so? – After a long pause, she asked him to get the
blueberry jam out of the kitchen for her, she had such a craving for
it. When he came back with spoon and jar, she was fast asleep.

He picked up his clothes, pinched out the candle flame, slunk out
of the room, and shut the door quietly behind him. He turned on
a light in the little living room. Then he got dressed. He found a
sheet of paper, and sat down at the desk.

 Nounou, I have to go. Who knows, perhaps by tomorrow it
would take a hundred knives to cut us apart, and the day after
a thousand. I promised myself the other day that I would try
and remain independent, and not participate in any storming of
heaven. I've used up all my parachutes. My damned brain sniffs
a dungheap behind every paradise. Adieu, Nounou, je t'embrasse.
Pansoti.

17.

Zündel hurried out of town in a northwesterly direction. He followed the winding coastal road that connects Rapallo and Santa Margherita. To the left lay the sea, gray and flat. It was three in the morning. – I feel like cheering, he thought, but I could also weep. Parting hurts, and it lightens the heart. Goodbyes weaken and ease.

In the little bay of San Michele he sat down on a stone bench, smoked and looked out at the sea. He tried not to think, so as not to have to think what – he supposed – anyone else would have thought in his shoes. So instead he tried to take in the world around him without words or thoughts, but soon realized he couldn't, wondered if others could, suddenly couldn't remember if a human being had four, five, six or seven senses, thought that was a disgrace, but perfectly symptomatic of this cerebral culture; thought this, thought that, jumped up and widdled spitefully into the sea.

Wandering on, he imagined sitting over breakfast with Nounou.

Nounou says: What about a game of something?

He says: Sure.

Nounou says: I'll ask you a question, and you have to answer it. If your answer is correct or in some other way pleasing, then I give you a match. And then you can ask me something. If my answer is correct or pleasing, then I get a match. The winner is the first to five.

He says: OK. You start!

Nounou asks: What is the strangest thing?

He answers: A long kiss with eyes open.

She pushes a match across to him.

He asks: How do you account for the fact that ninety-two of a hundred women say they prefer a man with a hairy chest?

Nounou answers: Because the other eight aren't telling the truth.

He pushes her two matches, but she gives one back.

She asks: Why is there fidelity?

He answers: Because of fear of the infidelity of the other.

Nounou says: Please expand!

He says: The faithful man is faithful because he is alarmed by the thought that infidelity on his part could provoke his partner to infidelity.

Half-true! says Nounou, and offers him half a match.

He asks: Why do most politicians resemble animals?

She answers: Because most of them are pigs, and the rest are wolves, foxes, vultures, geese, and centipedes.

Nounou is awarded a match.

She asks: What is the watchword of the Swiss?

He answers: There are several.

She says: Then tell me two.

He says: Firstly, experience everything and risk nothing. Second: always be packed and ready.

Nounou gives him a match.

He asks: How much bigger is the human egg than a human sperm?

She replies: Search me. Shall I have a guess?

Of course, he says generously. You can even have three guesses.

Twice as big?

No.

Eleven times?

No!

A hundred times bigger?

No, Nounou. No matches for you this time. An egg is eighty-five thousand times bigger than a sperm.

Mon dieu, exclaims Nounou impressed, what are we women doing wasting our time with little squirts like you.

Your turn, he says offended.

She asks: Why are there so many terms – including some really unpleasant ones – for diarrhea, and so few for constipation?

He answers: Because we are more in awe of the hyper-sensory.

Expand! she orders.

He says: What is visibly and olfactorily evident is talked to death, but what is discreet and not apparent elicits from us a mute respect.

I like it! says Nounou, and hands him a match.

He asks: What did the Americans call the Hiroshima bomb?

She answers: I don't know, and questions like that don't belong in this game.

He says: You're right, but I'll tell you anyway. The name of the bomb was 'Little Boy'.

You're making it up! screams Nounou.

It's the plain truth, he says.

She asks: Pansoti, why are there bad people?

He answers: I don't know.

She says: In that case, you haven't earned a single match.

Santa Margherita station, July 30, early morning:

But there's something else, dear Nounou, that I do know: more and more people are fed up. In my homeland for example, we have some citizens who carry banners saying: "Leave us alone!" They've had enough, they're fed up, but not fed up with bad things, but with protesting against the bad things! And in the lee of these opposition-weary people, blind by choice and desperate for peace, who identify their lost eyesight as optimism and their satiety as pleasure in existence, grimness grinning spreads, and calculates that not itself but its critics will be brought to book.

On the train to Genoa, July 30, 5:30:

Small resolution for those in want of rest:

We, all those in need of rest, hereby declare once and for all: a wild pandemonium of noisy pressure groups, know-it-alls, self-important self-appointed so-and-so's, chatterboxes, wild men, demagogues, bleaters, blowhards, and blatherers is forever tooting into the same stale horn and shouting their slogans out into the world, which would be a quieter, healthier, and more festive place without them. – We demand: Enough slander! Enough abuse of the planet! Enough of the self-righteous anti-creation talk! Enough with all the corrosive chitchat! – Let us be tolerant of the minor imperfections of this world, but we will not endure those notorious moaners who take themselves to be wiser than the Almighty and whose true purpose is to exchange their private woe for chaos for everyone.

Zündel bought cigarettes at a kiosk in the Genoa station. He drank a cup of coffee at a bar. Between the bottles ranked in front of a mirror at the bar, he caught his gray, alien face, and remembered his resolution to buy a revolver.

He was exhausted.

On the way to his pensione, he remarked at the cleanliness of the streets, which were just beginning to come to life. Like eyes clanging open, sliding shutters were pulled up.

Zündel slept till evening.

A little before seven he got up, drank some water and thought:

What do I do now?

He clipped his fingernails.

Today's Thursday, he thought.
Tomorrow's Friday.
I'm not hungry.
If I wore glasses, I would clean them now.

He went back to bed.
   At midnight he woke up, bathed in sweat and shivering.
   He turned on the light.
   A dream. I'm hanging on a cliff face. The rescue helicopter hovering in front of me. At the controls is my father, eyeing me calmly. Then he veers away.

18.

Apart from occasional breaches of traffic regulations and two or three joyrides on the Zürich public transport system, Zündel had never yet perpetrated any serious infraction of the law. So much the bolder he now seemed to himself, stalking through the streets early on Friday evening, resolved to take the plunge. It was time to get the revolver. What good to him was the venerable carbine in the cupboard at home which he never touched except when he had to? No, what he needed now was a handgun, and preferably a revolver, a plain little common-or-garden revolver. – A pistol wasn't quite the thing. Pistols have magazines, and ever since recruit school, Zündel hadn't got along with magazines. (On the second or third day the new recruits had been drilled in the use of the assault rifle – in particular the fitting of the magazine – and of the whole company there were only two recruits, who – instructed by a despairing lieutenant – lay there in the barracks corridor until far at night practicing, incapable, apparently, of mastering the simple knack: namely Zündel and a blatant cretin by the name of Bölsterli, who was allowed to go home after a week.)

A revolver, then. According to the dictionary, una revoltella. – Una revoltella con cinquanta colpi. With fifty bullets.

The fellow who had just hissed "Hashish!" in Zündel's ear is the right sort: strong jawline, unshaven, flashing eyes – a proper hoodlum.

Zündel stops and says quietly but firmly: Una revoltella.

The fellow doesn't bat an eyelid, just whispers: Follow me, but keep a distance.

He steers Zündel into one of the many little lanes connecting the Via di Prè with the Via Gramsci, the harbor road, none of them much wider than four feet or so.

Zündel pays careful attention: the name of the little lane is Vico dell'Amore, and at the bottom end of it, shortly before it joins the harbor road, there's a public convenience. The man draws up, stands there feet apart, pretending. He nods to Zündel to come nearer. Zündel stands next to him, and he too pretends to pee.

The fellow says: Name's Carlo, you can trust me. Up ahead on the harbor road, a couple of hundred yards, left-hand side, you'll find a gun shop. You go ahead, look the display, I remain in sight.

Zündel thinks these precautions are a bit overdone, but it is Carlo, and not himself who is the expert in criminal etiquette.

So he sets off, and thinks of Serafino, with whom he strolled here arm in arm.

The first prostitutes are already leaning against house fronts and parked cars.

Here is the gun shop.

He glances at the models in the window display and in spite of the variety on offer, he quickly plumps for a neat, silver revolver, a 38 special, with brown wooden inlays in the handle.

He motions to Carlo who is standing some twenty yards away in conversation with someone. Carlo strolls up and says half-loud: OK, quick! Which one you want? – At the back on the right, 38 special, 200,000 lire, con cinquanta colpi, whispers Zündel. – All right, says Carlo, now my colleague take you to a safe place. I get gun you want and come in half hour. OK?

The other man, his colleague, looks even shadier than Carlo. Zündel isn't happy about being in the care of two criminals. But he trots along at a little distance behind his new guide.

Again, they dive into little alleyways, reach the Via di Prè, follow it down a little way, then turn right into a lane full of garbage, which before terminating in the lively Via Balbi spreads out into a little square.

There they wait.

There is no conversation.

They smoke.

Way up, on a clothesline hanging across the piazza a few items of laundry hang motionlessly.

I don't stand a chance, thinks Zündel. One of them grabs me, and the other takes my money off me, and if I resist at all, they beat me to death. I can't bale out of it either – of course, that's why Carlo gave me this guard. Christ, what a bloody beginner I am, walking into this trap. Death with dignity – that's what it was about. But to perish miserably in some shitty Genoese alleyway, I really didn't deserve that!

It starts getting dark.

His guard is humming to himself innocently.

Finally, Carlo turns up, the parcel with weapon and rounds under his arm. The box is wrapped in brown packing paper, and tied with string, more than once.

Zündel is ashamed of his suspicion.

The accomplice is detailed to stand at the bottom of the lane and keep a look out over Via Balbi.

Then Carlo says: 200,000 and 50,000 for the risk. The bullets – no charge. OK?

Zündel stares in horror at Carlo's left hand: he is missing an index finger, the stump is taped up with a soiled plaster.

No agree? asks Carlo.

Yes, of course, 250,000, OK, OK! says Zündel and reaches for his wallet. Then he hesitates. And says: Don't get me wrong, but perhaps I could look at it before I pay?

Carlo reaches out, thumps Zündel heartily on the back, holds out the parcel to him, and says: Bravo, I see you understand the bees' knees! Do you see the bar across the road, next to the cartoleria? Go in, and go through the swing doors at the back, and on the right you see a small WC. There you open the package in peace. You pay afterward, I wait here.

Zündel takes a few steps toward the Via Balbi, and looks uncertainly at the road. He thinks: the fact that Carlo has encouraged me to check means that my checking is actually unnecessary, and the fact that he lets me go without asking for his money upfront proves that even in the so-called criminal underworld there is still such a thing as personal trust.

So he turns and goes back to Carlo and says with a twinkle: Oh, I expect you've got me the right one!

He thanks Carlo for his engagement with a shake of the hand and counts twenty-five banknotes into the three-fingered hand.

Carlo whistles up his accomplice.

The two of them natter incomprehensibly.

The accomplice disappears up the lane, Carlo thumps Zündel on the back once more, and invites him to have a drink.

Zündel is anxious to get back to his room, and Carlo's presence makes him feel somehow at risk, but he doesn't want to be unfriendly.

Very well, the Pippo Bar is nearby, they drink a Cynar together, the parcel remains wedged under Zündel's arm, they chat, Carlo praises Zündel's Italian, and he's just an all-round nice guy. At the finish, he warns him off the other black marketeers, there were some pretty insalubrious types among them.

Carlo offers to pay, but Zündel says decisively: No, no, I'm paying, this is my treat, you've done me a great service after all.

Outside he shakes Carlo's hoodlum paw once more, thanks him again, and then he walks more cheerfully than for weeks to his albergo.

He really felt he was on his way to a date, that's how flushed his cheeks were, how expectantly his pulse was beating. In addition there was his satisfaction at having safely mastered a not everyday set of challenges. Everything had gone so well, when it could so easily have gone wrong!

He locked the door.

He laid the parcel on the bed and straightaway sawed through the string with his penknife. Then he undid the packing paper, saw that the box was further wrapped in some sheets of newspaper, removed those, unpeeled four strips of masking tape that were laid round the box, and – with a feeling of tenderness that surprised him – lifted the lid. There, on a bed of green wood wool, lay a chunk of plaster of Paris. White and ceremonial.

Zündel clasped his bottom with both hands. Only great self-control kept him from wailing at the top of his voice. He stamped three times and ground his teeth. Then he slumped down on to the bed next to the box, and said, aloud: What a moron I am! – Still more loudly he said: I'm the most feeble-witted asshole in the world. I've had enough. I'm not just naïve and unworldly, I am plainly and simply a bloody imbecile.

He took the shapeless and heavy lump of plaster in his hand, looked at it and murmured: I see, a .38 special, I see.

Then, just to be sure, he reached into the wood-wool, just exactly like a still dissatisfied child will reach into its Easter egg nest, to see if there might not be a little extra surprise. But all he found was an empty cartridge.

He managed a polite laugh.

For a long time he sat on the bed.

His rage and disappointment gradually abated, shame was more obdurate.

By half past ten there was nothing in him but cold indifference and a little sorrow that he was unable to see any humor in his experience.

My sense of humor has gone, he thought. Hunger has left me, humor has left me, my wife has left me, the Colt never even came. In my mouth I've got a chunky provisional tooth, on my face a potato nose, and in my heel a sea-urchin prong slowly going septic. Meanwhile, not far away, a couple of gangsters are sitting eating and drinking and cracking up about the klutz they've milked. Such is life. Today's Friday. Tomorrow's Saturday. The day after tomorrow I won't be going to Tripoli, I'm going home, because the holiday is over, and I am what I was and always will be, which is to say a dutiful and submissive individual.

19.

At six in the morning he was already wide-awake. He folded his hands behind his head, and gazed up at the ceiling.

The quest is at an end, he thought. You could believe the source of depression was in the sum of all misfortunes. But against that there is the fact that a hundred misfortunes aren't enough to rob a life-affirming fellow of his affirmativeness. So if joie de vivre exists in spite of and including misfortunes, surely there is also an absence of joie de vivre that operates independently of misfortunes.

(By the bye: why are those people who have everything and still manage to be unhappy not less well thought of than those who have nothing and still manage to be happy? Both could use an explanation, but only the unhappy fellow is asked to account for himself.)

Where was I? – Yes, if there is a dejection without misfortunes on the one hand and on the other – thinking of myself now – one freighted with misfortunes, then, then – oh, crap! But I don't mind slowly growing stupid. It could even be that all these curses and minor afflictions are not the cause for my state of soul, but its consequence. Perhaps my make-up makes me receptive to those facts that best explain my makeup. Perhaps my lack of joie de vivre has specialized in finding unjoyful things, so as not to appear unmotivated, to clear up mysteries, to keep the quest from ending.

So. Hans gets the flu. Fritz doesn't. A question of susceptibility, as everyone knows. The flu goes after Hans, because Hans doesn't resist it. The flu doesn't cause Hans's weak resistance. But it will intensify his sense of frailty.

We are asking after the causes of Hans's weakness.

The cause of his vital consciousness.

Why is Fritz happy?

Fritz doesn't go hungry or thirsty, he isn't cold, he has an apartment, a job, everything.

Same with Hans.

Why is Hans unhappy (even when he hasn't got the flu)?

There are some causes of contemporary unhappiness that are referred to as syndromes, because they are so overly familiar: Concrete architecture. Violence. Anonymity. Coldness. Competition. Bad air. Bad water. Noise. The A-bomb. The B-bomb. The C-bomb.

But Fritz is subject to all of them too – and he's still happy!

A pachyderm?

And Hans the sensitive one? The one with the translucent skin?

Then all problems are basically skin-deep? A happy life is a matter of dermatology?

How come Hans has his unfit-for-purpose skin, and Fritz his thick pelt?

Dunno.

Just that it forms part of the strategy of the unscrupulous to persuade the despondent that they are responsible for their skin type, and should curse not the world but themselves. They need to understand that they are moaners, and should be ashamed of their grief. They should kindly take themselves off, and leave the world to the wolves. But if the grief-stricken go, then it's not just Mary the comforter who will die as well, but all sense of things being amiss. If the patient dies, the causes of death are buried with him. If the sufferers go to the wall, the weak efface themselves, and the mad are confined, then the world is as it should be, then positive thoughts will reign, and no sounds will challenge the resounding, roly-poly hallelujahs of the competent.

I'm so fed up with these thoughts, I wish I had a calmer brain. I'm lying in bed, protesting. A recumbent protester is what I am. And even that's too much for me. Outside, I'm quieter. It's indoors that I begin to make a racket. And in bed I'm positively fearless. But that's too much for me now. I want to be quiet inside and out, not well-behaved, not courageous, just quiet. Quiet like a bag of trash by the side of the road, waiting to be picked up.

When Konrad straightened up, he felt dizzy, and when he stood up he realized his legs could hardly carry him. Even the thought of a sandwich made him feel sick.

Somewhere he tossed down a couple of brandies, standing up. Eight o'clock found him in a hairdresser's salon – the day's first customer – where he asked the barber to cut his hair as short as possible.

A number four? asked the hairdresser. – Number one! said Konrad. He felt a little embarrassed that his stomach was growling so loud, but before long he heard the hairdresser's stomach growling too, and he followed their duet with fascination.

With even greater fascination – albeit with growing horror – he watched the remorseless metamorphosis of his head in the mirror. At the end of twenty minutes he saw himself confronting a creature for which he had no feeling at all.

Whatever that is, it's not a human head, he thought, it's like the cross between a plucked pheasant and a darning egg. Magda would be rigid with shock if she saw me. But there won't be anyone in the apartment tomorrow night. The family silver that Magda brought as a dowry will be gone too, so that I'll be sitting at the kitchen table, glad of my penknife to smear a slice of moldy bread with rancid butter.

Konrad bought a bottle of cognac and went up to his room. From ten in the morning till midnight he wrote.

Then – on shaky legs – he went out for a walk. On the main harbor road there was still some activity, but all the alleyways were deserted. Konrad felt scared. When he suddenly noticed a dark shape lying in front of him, he began to shake all over. If that's a human being, he thought, I'm going to fold up. – It was a dog, and Konrad said in relief: Rest in peace, brother. – Back in his room, he looked in the mirror and again failed to recognize himself.

Better a dead dog than a living lion, he thought.

Then he went on writing, until five in the morning.

Last entry:

On Dignity

"Dignity" – isn't that the desperate effort, in view of our nugatoriness, to maintain our posture? And is that a good thing?

Misery must be branded, frailty must be indicated so that the heavenly hosts finally rally to us. As long as we are struggling for dignity, they will think we are well.

At noon on Sunday, Konrad stood on the station square taking one last look at Christopher Columbus. Only now did he notice that Columbus's left hand was resting on a mighty anchor, while his right was caressing the neck of a mermaid sitting at his feet.

By nine o'clock that evening, Konrad was home.

20.

I reprise: on the morning of July 9, a Thursday, Zündel had taken the cat round to Judith, and told her he was "going South." On Saturday (July 11), Magda had returned home after a stay in Bern (with her friend Helen). She had looked in vain for her cat or a message from Konrad, and that night her efforts to shake off her deep disquiet and get some sleep had been similarly vain. (It was as though she had some psychic sense that her husband – pursued by two policemen – had been running down the lanes of Genoa, till brought up short by a metal chain.)

On Sunday, Magda had called various friends, myself among them. I told her about Konrad's visit to me (on Tuesday, the night of July 7), but kept from her, so as not to make her still more anxious, the dreadful state he was in. (A state that – as we know from Konrad's own notes – was only made worse by his janitor-Schmocker-induced fear of unfaithfulness on her part.) – Judith, however, when she was called by Magda, kept nothing back, but told her alarmed friend in excited detail how awful Konrad had looked when he had brought the cat round to her place, deathly pale, whey-faced, like a ghost, etc. and he had talked like a madman, she had been terrified, and asked him what was the matter, etc., etc.

After this information Magda could only fear the worst.

It was a shock to her to hear how tragically Konrad seemed to have reacted to their difference of opinion and her flight to Bern. She loved him! She clung to him. But for all that, she had been looking forward to getting a couple of weeks by herself. She had just been caught off guard by his early return, and hadn't managed to respond except with impatience and irritation. It's not possible always to be loving, sometimes one has the right to withdraw from the other, to deny him the understanding he expects, and to refuse his claim of intimacy. Konrad's words! Words that Magda now remembered, without her feeling of guilt being any the less for it.

The following days ground her down. She waited. Ran down to the letterbox day after day. Nothing but junk mail.

She hardly dared leave the house, for fear that Konrad might return while she happened to be out.

If she went to the shops, she left an especially doting welcome note on the kitchen table, and a chocolate éclair beside it – they were a great passion of his, even though he never admitted it.

Once, she went swimming. Once to the cinema with Judith. And once she went to the Aargau to her mother-in-law, because she wanted to be with someone who was close to Konrad.

Magda admired Johanna Zündel at the same time as feeling slightly afraid of this unconventional woman who had raised her son alone and managed to give him love that was free of the usual devouring tendency. The fact that she had had to relinquish the father of her child could never induce her to sink her hooks into the child and go to him for everything she had been denied by his father. In fact, all things demanding, rapacious, greedy, and anxiously adhesive were foreign to her nature. And when Konrad and Magda married, Johanna had said to her daughter-in-law: Look after him, but don't lock him up. – And to her son, whose fear of life she could sense, she said: Don't expect too much of your wife, don't turn her into your refuge!

Johanna radiated such serenity, such unshowy maturity, that Magda felt terribly young and flawed when she was with her.

But the visit did her good. His mother didn't know anything about Konrad's whereabouts either, but she was able to make Magda a little more optimistic, and take away some of her fears. Above all, Johanna wasn't having any guilt from her daughter-in-law. Women – she thought – tend to have pangs of conscience as soon as they detect feelings in themselves that don't sit with the ideal of devotion. The basic form of the relationship of a man and a woman – thus Johanna – since the time of Odysseus had the man going off to the wars or going bowling when he wanted to be without his wife, but assuming at the same time she would be sitting over her knitting till he got back; she had no need to spread her wings and do anything without her husband. She, Johanna, had always wished her son an affectionate but not submissive companion, and she had done everything in her power to protect Konrad from the usual, somewhat sadistic stereotype of woman. Moreover, she had tried to relativize his sense of manhood – thus influencing him from both directions – and she was glad she had, even if she could see he might feel a little weak and "unmanly."

I refuse to raise a child, said Johanna, in conformity with something I have identified as bad, just so that he has an easier time of it. That's not in my gift. I'd rather take the blame for having inadequately prepared him for so-called life. I bear some responsibility, I know. But isn't it also guilt of a kind if you raise your child to be a reliable participant and perpetuator of idiocy? The question is, what do we want our children to be, reasonably contented accomplices or unhappy resistance fighters? What do you think?

Magda said: How about a happy resistance fighter!

As I say, the visit to her mother-in-law did Magda good, she felt lighter and stronger afterward, and when Konrad's postcard, postmarked the 18, arrived from Genoa a couple of days later, on July 24, Magda felt a rush of relief. What he wrote was bizarre, but at least he was alive.

She thought about him a lot. Was he really – for all Johanna's efforts – not just a typical man, with all the foibles that she, Magda, with the help of her women's group, had learned to identify so thoroughly? Did she not regularly feel herself oppressed, leaned on, hobbled? Was she not sometimes afraid of his judgment? Did he not seek to dominate her? Why should she feel guilty when she was in the mood to go out and he was tired? And what if she actually did – it hardly ever happened – go out alone or with friends? Did all that not indicate that he was just another chauvinist?

Could she on the other hand forget how her parents had tied her down? Could that not be why she was so sensitive on that score? And more: was it not conceivable that she was subconsciously blurring Konrad with her parents, and trying to attribute to his forbidding voice what in reality was the voice of her parents still echoing around inside her? Wasn't it possible that it was this voice and not Konrad at all that called for her subjugation, and talked her into feeling guilty on those occasions when she felt like going out and he was tired? And if she actually did – it hardly ever happened – go without him, as he had often enough encouraged her to do, then was it fair of her to hate him for it, and give him the blame for her guilt feelings?

Magda havered, she wasn't sure how things really stood, and she thought every effort to analyze a relationship had something oddly random about it, and that even the most illuminating theories actually didn't deserve any better than a shake of the head and some pity.

She felt closer to Konrad than ever.

Toward the end of the last week of the holidays her concern grew. Hitherto, Konrad had always used the last days of the holidays to prepare for the school term ahead. No matter how idyllic things were in Provence or wherever they might be: at the very latest four days before the start of classes they had to leave, and once he was home again, Konrad couldn't be prised away from his desk. That he might one day simply slough off his exaggerated sense of duty was something Magda thought desirable but hardly likely.

And now it was Saturday, August 1.* In the evening there was a women's group meeting, followed by a festive trip out to the lake, but Magda had said she wasn't going.

She felt nervous. Each time a firecracker went off outside, she jumped. There was a lot of noise all day, and even though Magda had become familiar with the rowdy style of patriotism hereabouts, it almost drove her mad.

So the national holiday passed without Konrad, but then at nine o'clock on Saturday night – as already stated – there he was suddenly standing in the doorway.

---

* *Translator's note*: August 1st is the Swiss national holiday, the equivalent to the Fourth of July and the Quatorze Juillet and all the rest of them.

21.

There is no other way of putting it: Magda was rigid with shock. And as for Konrad's appearance, one has to say it was pitiful.

Apart from the darker patches of stubble, his face was ghostly pale. The brow especially, lengthened by the recent brutal haircut, looked waxen. His lantern jaws transformed his appearance. His cheekbones bulged, and the eyes were sunk in their hollows, the look in them was one she had never seen.

There he stood, haggard, awkward, silent, smelling of sweat and booze.

Finally, almost inaudibly, he asked the stunned Magda: What are *you* doing here?

Waiting for you! she cried, threw her arms round him, crying, and pressed him to her. My God I've missed you, I was so worried for you, my poor dear husband!

Konrad did not hold her, but nor did he try to break away either, he just stood there with his arms hanging down, and said: There there.

Magda pulled him into the living room.

Come on, come, what's the matter with you, what's the matter with you for Lord's sake? Are you ill? Yes, you're ill, what's the matter with you?

The sole of my foot is poisoned, said Konrad, apart from that I'm all right, but I stink.

He said little, and didn't talk about what he had been through.

Magda was careful of him. She avoided asking him questions. Luckily, he agreed to eat a little something, and he didn't refuse a bubble bath either. She sat on the edge of the tub, stroking his head, and said: I like your new haircut.

He said: There there.

Tomorrow morning, Magda said, I'll call the school and tell them you're not well. Then I'll nurse you back to health.

Konrad asked: Did your brother leave?

Oh, Koni, she said, you know I don't have a brother! Since when did you think I had a brother?

I see, he said, absent-mindedly.

Magda didn't show her horror at Konrad's confusion. She said: Guess what, I've started smoking, I think it was purely from missing you so badly! Did you think of me sometimes when you were in Italy? – Yes, he said.

After his bath, he seemed to feel better. In his dressing gown he sat down at the table, and drank a chamomile tea. He asked: Did she get a new lampshade then? – That's not new, Magda contradicted him, we always had that! – Konrad said: It shed a kindlier light before. – She changed the subject: Guess what, I knitted a new sweater vest for you – wouldn't you like to try it on? – He said: Summer's all very well, but what about the flies. – Come on, just try it on for me, said Magda, you can keep your pajama top on. – He took off his dressing gown, and she brought the vest for him to slip into. After a while he said: That's not possible. – Magda said: But why not, it's a lovely fit, don't you like it? Konrad said: Can't you hear the wind whistling through it.

Fighting off laughter and tears, Magda lit a cigarette. Then she said: Well, is it all right if I call tomorrow and tell the school you're ill? – No! he cried, that's all I need! I've only got two classes tomorrow, both history, and a break in between, I can manage that! – Are you prepared? asked Magda. He answered: For thirty-two years I was industrious and dependable. Where idleness dwells, the beams sag – or so I thought. Well, I was a busy carle, and they sagged anyway.

Tears slithered down his expressionless face. Magda put her

arms around him, and said quietly: Come on, I'll put you to bed!
– I still need to pack my briefcase, he said.

He stood in front of the bookcase, pulled out the odd volume,
leafed around in it, and put it back. One blue paperback he kept
in his hands for longer. – Listen to this, Magda! he suddenly said.
– Yes, I'm listening. – He read: "Of course life is poor and solitary.
We live in the depths, like the diamond in its pit. In vain do we
ask how we got there, in the hope of making our way back up."

He went on browsing, and asked: Are you listening? – Yes,
darling, she replied. He read: "When I see a child and think how
humiliating and deleterious is the yoke it will bear, and that it
will work, as we do, that it will seek people, as we do, to ask, as
we do, after the beautiful and the true, that it will pass infertile,
that it – O, pluck your sons out of their cradles, and throw them
in the river . . ."

Nice, isn't it? said Konrad, but Magda said: I want a baby!
– Now, all at once? he asked. – Yes, she replied, for the last two
weeks I've wanted a baby.

Silently, he stowed a couple of books in his briefcase. He
asked: Do you know what the time is? – Ten to midnight, she
said, are you sure you want me to wake you at half past six? –
Whatever for? he murmured, and, because Magda was looking
at him questioningly: I'm never going to set foot in that fiendish
establishment again! – Good, she said, then we can have a lie in
tomorrow morning.

He went to the bathroom once more. When he came back, he
said sadly: Toilet paper is getting shoddier by the day.

Do you want to be by yourself? she asked shyly, and he
answered: It's probably advisable.

Magda saw him to his room, and tucked him up. Konrad
whispered: I can't find him in any of the encyclopedias! – Find
who? she asked. – A man by the name of John Knickerbocker! –
Who's that? – He's the author of a little sentence I greatly admire,

replied Konrad, even though it's only three words long.

Magda waited patiently for the sentence to be vouchsafed to her, but soon noticed that Konrad had fallen into a deep sleep.

Later she lay in bed, crying. She felt as though she had someone's knee pressed against her throat.

Shortly after six she was woken by a jangle of glassware. She got up right away. Konrad was sitting at the table, fully dressed. His hands were shaking. In front of him was a large glass brimful of brandy. – You're not drinking that! screamed Magda. – I am drinking that, said Konrad in hoarse tones, I have to drink that, because otherwise I won't be able to teach. – She dropped onto the sofa and said: You're mad. – He picked up the glass, and drained it. Then he said: You see how calm my hands are now, you used to be so keen on them once, do you remember, these hands? – I still love them, sobbed Magda, but you mustn't destroy yourself, please please stay at home, you're so ill, I want to look after you and make you better, I love you! – Konrad said: I was your diving board, and you were my Dutch tiled stove, and both were wrong, and both were a mistake. – That's a lie! cried Magda, you were never my diving board, and if I was your Dutch stove, then it's because I liked it! – You're lying, roared Konrad, you should be ashamed of yourself, Schmocker told me everything! – What did he tell you, that slimy so-and-so! – Oh, all sorts of things, said Konrad, but we're not talking about them anymore, they're all over and in the past, now we have to take things as they come. Thank you for your farewell letter! – What farewell letter? asked Magda. – The one you left on the kitchen table, before you went to Bern to see Helen, went to Bern to see Helen, a comprehensive list of my character flaws. – Oh, God! said Magda, please understand, please forgive me! – There's nothing to forgive, he said, you were absolutely right, I was a monster, but you too are just flesh and blood and other shortcomings, and it's quite possible that neither of us will get into heaven. I'm cold, you be warm. – I'm here, said Magda, and she stood up and despairingly kissed his pallid face.

Konrad went to school.

Magda hadn't been able to keep him at home.

He had spent a long time standing in front of the bathroom mirror, saying the same line twenty or thirty times in a row, that she – Magda – would never forget: "On the brows of a man thrones queen Duty."

22.

Before the beginning of classes, Zündel sat in the teachers' common room, staring into space, apparently intent on not being spoken to by anyone. He wasn't completely able to evade the general round of handshaking that went on, but if a colleague ventured a comment on his new haircut, then a stone-faced Zündel turned away.

The kids giggled. One asked whether he – Zündel – had fallen under a tram. Another asked if he had had to repeat recruit school, or was converting to Buddhism.

It was all good-natured banter.

But no smiling here either! Zündel kept silent till the class fell silent, and every last one of them sensed that the man standing rigidly in front of them was in no mood for pleasantries.

Finally Zündel said softly: Watch out, you watch out, no one is blessed from the womb, and a pair of shears will come for every head.

Then he sat down and pulled two books out of his briefcase. – I will begin by reacquainting you, he said, with the seventeenth century. Fresh and well-rested and nut-brown as we all are, we will tackle the Thirty Years' War. But first I need to attune you, to familiarize you with the sensibility of a bygone age of suffering, an age that is also a valedictory age, because it is the last that would not allow life to pull the wool over its eyes, that declined to wallow in the mire of false optimism. Verily, grisly things have happened since. Two global conflagrations in our century alone. And the third wiping its feet at the door. Meanwhile humanity, sunk in ever deeper gruntlement, worships at the altar of positivism, adores the doddering politicians who steer our destinies and stride around and shout and rattle their sabers only because they want to displace death. They survive as long as they project strength! And humanity the same, besotted with muscles, adores iron and steel and concrete and all things that are durable and hard and less transient than we ourselves. – Are you familiar with the neutron bomb? Yes? Did you know it is a product of modern love? A product of that worship of which I spoke a moment ago? Are you aware that it – this innocent snowflake of a weapon – will spare the bunker and the tower block, the motorway and the runway, and will confine itself to the annihilation of frail Mother Nature? – Well, there was a time when man was not ashamed of his infirmity, when he did not seek to cover over his forked nugatoriness either with body building or with cruise missiles, when man dared to see himself in his full wretched frailty. – And it is of this time that we will today speak. We will listen to two witnesses from this time.

Zündel made a long pause. Then he opened the first of the two books he had brought with him.

He said: I will read a few words from our first witness, kindly open your ears to him.

He read: "I know not who put me into the world, nor what the world is, nor what I myself am. I am in terrible ignorance of everything. I know not what my body is, nor my senses, nor my soul, not even that part of me which thinks what I say, which reflects on all and on itself, and knows itself no more than the rest. I see those frightful spaces of the universe which surround me, and I find myself tethered to one corner of this vast expanse, without knowing why I am put in this place rather than in another, nor why the short time which is given me to live is assigned to me at this point rather than at another of the whole eternity which was before me or which shall come after me. I see nothing but infinites on all sides, which surround me as an atom and as a shadow which endures only for an instant and returns no more. All I know is that I must soon die, but what I know least is this very death which I cannot escape. As I know not whence I come, so I know not whither I go."

Zündel set the book down, made another long pause, then reached for the other book and said: I will read a few words from our second witness, kindly open your ears to him!

He read: "Adieu, O! World, for in thee cannot be trusted, from thee is nothing to hope; in thy house the past is already vanished, the present vanishes under our hands, the future has never begun; the all secure falls, the all strong breaks, the all eternal comes to an end; so that thou art dead among the dead, and in a hundred years sufferest us to live not an hour. For here every man crieth, waileth, groaneth, lamenteth and is undone. In thy house one sees and learns only to hate to the point of asphyxiation, to talk to the point of lying, to love to the point of despairing, and to sin to the point of dying. –

"May God stand by thee, world, because thy conversation vexeth me; the life thou givest us is a wretched pilgrimage, an inconstant, uncertain, hard, rough, fleeting and unclean life, full of poverty and error; it is to be called death rather than life; for we all die in it every moment, through the many frailties of inconstancy and the manifold ways of death. From the golden chalice that thou holdest in thy hands thou givest us bitterness and falsehood to drink, and makest us blind, deaf, mad, drunk and without reason. Thou makest of us a dark abyss, a miserable clod of earth, a child of fury, a stinking carrion; for when thou hast long beset us with flattery, caresses, urgings, blows, plagues, tribulations, martyrdom and pain, then thou givest the ill-used body unto the grave. But woe then unto the poor soul that has served and obeyed Thee, O World!'"*

Hereupon – visibly exhausted – Zündel clapped the book shut, and even though the bell was fully twenty minutes away, he stood up and said: Here endeth the lesson. – He picked up his briefcase and walked slowly out the door.

The ensuing free period found him again sitting silently in the common room.

He tied four knots in his handkerchief, one in each corner. Then he found a cork in his trouser pocket and sniffed at it. – Nearby two German teachers were in conversation. – I have, said the one, I have used the holidays to reacquaint myself with Goethe's Sesenheimer poems, and I must say, it was a real treat. My wife found them accessible as well.

Suddenly Zündel spoke up. Aloud. So loud that everyone else in the room fell silent. He said: I hope your principal access to your wife isn't bunged up with poems, that would be a pity.

His colleague looked at him with utter blankness. Zündel however – ignoring the general embarrassment – spoke on. He asked: Do you know what a tanga is? – You mean tango? his colleague replied politely. – No, cried Zündel, I don't mean tango, I mean tanga!

Now Dr. Wipp, a geography master sitting two tables away, joined in the conversation, and said: Tanga is a port city in Tanzania in east Africa, at the beginning of the so-called Tanga rail line, which leads to Kilimanjaro!

The assembled teachers were astounded. Zündel said impressed: Very good, Herr Wipp, very well informed. My question though,

---

Translator's note: From Grimmelshausen's *Simplicissimus*; the previous quotation is from Pascal. The translator thanks the author for the information in both cases.

was, what *a* tanga was, and that's not the way you would ask a question about a city, is it now? So I'm afraid I can't give you top marks for your answer, Herr Wipp. No, no, gentlemen, tanga – *a* tanga – is something else, namely a sophisticated form of ladies' underwear that leaves the buttocks bare, a cheeky minimalist symphony of satin and tulle, also available in lace – that's what a tanga is!

And returning to the German teacher, he said: Why don't you buy her one of those, who knows, maybe it'll animate your arid Sesenheimer sex life!

Deathly silence.

The colleague thus addressed, in consternation but calmly, finally asked: What's the matter with you, Konrad?

Someone else, further off, asked: Are you crazy?

Oswald, an English teacher and a good friend of Zündel's, jumped up, clasped him by the shoulder, and said: Koni, come on, what's the matter, aren't you feeling well? I'll take you home.

But Zündel, evidently not in control of himself, shook Oswald off, and shouted: Don't you act so sanctimonious, you bunch of pricks, you rancid humanists, you purple bumfaces, you poor, pathetic, deceitful, perverted pedagogical shits, you smeary peddlers, you blinkered purveyors of ignorance – can't you hear it ringing?

He picked up his briefcase and ran out of the room.

Of those left behind, not one doubted that their generally so reticent, yes, buttoned-up colleague had lost his mind. But no one was willing to go after him and spare him the next lesson.

It was a senior class, consisting of just fifteen pupils with which Zündel had his final lesson, a class he generally liked teaching.

Good holidays? he asked, then without waiting for a reply, he continued: I take it there isn't anyone sitting in these halls who thinks our seven State Councilors are not just boring old farts as we often get to hear, but cunning and unscrupulous evildoers?

The pupils looked at Zündel in bewilderment. What perplexed them wasn't so much his question, which they failed to understand right away on account of its construction, as the term "halls" for their seminar room, which was one of the smallest in the building.

Well? asked Zündel.

Someone raised his hand and asked: Would you mind repeating the question, sir?

Zündel thought about it for a while, and finally replied: No, that's asking too much of me. Nor was I asking a question as such. But one thing I will say to you: Be on your guard! Beware of fraternizing with reality! As soon as you come to an accommodation with it, be it out of a desire to lean on something, be it the wish to get ahead in life, you're done for. And do you know why? The real and the divine were once one and the same thing. But the history of the world is a process of mangling. And today it is Satan who is sitting on the last, remotest tip of reality, which therefore has become one and the same as the diabolical! – What is the contemporary CV? Nauseating. Nauseating in three acts. Three acts, like a comedy. Act One: Rebellion against the pre-existent, i.e., evil. Act Two: Adjustment to the existing, i.e., evil. Act Three: Affirmation of the existing, i.e., evil. – But I forget, the language of truth is unfamiliar to you. You've learned it this way: Act One: Pubescent idealism. Act Two: Maturity. Act Three: Completion of maturity, wisdom, serenity. That's the way you learned it, and so for you there is nothing more desirable than to be intimate with the real, which is to say the diabolical. So you sit on these benches year after year, staring into the grim features of hopeless trainers, and listening to the spastic feeblemindedness that falls from their lips. Has it not dawned on you that all your teachers, among whom for purposes of argument I include your parents, are nothing but crooked pimps and procurers, seeking to drive you, come what may, into the arms of reality? And do you want to know their method? – Fear! They frighten you with orders, instructions, grades, punishments, humiliation, with pressure, duress, threat and loss of love. Education is nothing but the deliberate, persistent, inexhaustible production of fear, and whoever would seek to deny that is a corrupt sonofabitch, and is crying out for treatment with red hot irons! – But what do you do meanwhile with the chronic fears that have been bred into you? – There is only one way, one method, to get rid of them: self-subjugation, assimilation, identification with the tormentors, the yelped Oh yes! to your own mutilation, the French kiss with the status quo, the ostentatious coupling with reality. – I should like to be more emphatic here, stuff it in your pipes and smoke it: existence is dying to be fucked by you, and your teachers would like nothing better than to watch you at it. And the more enthusiastically you go about it, the more relaxed, benevolent, radiant is the expression on their faces. – That's just the way it is. End of story. – And so our lesson has come to a natural end, and it would be craven to wait for a bell to ring.

Zündel made to leave the room, but missed the door handle several times.

He turned back to the class which was sitting there in silent bewilderment, and said quietly: They're trying to lock me up. Note the double meaning.

With that he tottered back to his desk, sat down, and wrote in his class log: Nothing out of the ordinary.

His face turned pale, his features grew sharp, suddenly he vomited. He tried to get up, probably to run to a washbasin, pushed himself upright, smiled, said "Hup!" and again "Hup!" and slumped down in a heap.

23.

For two days he lay in the hospital, unresponsive, stiff, but with eyes almost continually open.

The results of the usual diagnostic tests were only alarming in that they failed to turn up indications for any specific condition. His blood values were normal, his urine unexceptional, his temperature within the standard range. There were no stools. His undernourishment was hardly sufficient cause for his behavior, and an initial suspicion of chronic alcohol poisoning was rejected.

The sisters and doctors kept talking to him, asking him questions, but he remained silent.

Magda visited him every day, he seemed to see through her. He ignored his mother as well.

He took no notice of me.

He was fed intravenously.

On the morning of the third day, a big medical round. A phalanx of a dozen doctors, from the chief internist to the junior trainee, bunched round Zündel's bed.

You do the honors! said the chief surgeon to Dr. Hunkeler. Dr. Hunkeler described the case a little ponderously but confidently enough. Among other things, he observed that the patient was incapable of speech, though his hearing seemed to be intact. Hereupon the chief surgeon interrupted: What do you mean, "seems to be intact"? Is it intact or isn't it? – Hunkeler scratched his throat. Zündel looked at him and said amiably: Hi there, Rölfli!

The whole group jumped, whether it was the unexpected return of Zündel's gift of speech, or whether they all knew that Hunkeler's given name was indeed Rolf.

Dr. Hunkeler, quite discombobulated, asked stammeringly: Do you know me then?

And into the profound silence, Zündel said: Sure, you're Rölfli. You always used to wet your pants!

Ward sister Gertrud, standing near the back, wasn't able to get her handkerchief out in time, and whinnied loudly.

A second later the whole group was rocking with mirth.

The next day Zündel was transferred to a psychiatric clinic.

PSYCHIATRIST: So you're Herr Zündel, then?

ZÜNDEL: To order.

PSYCHIATRIST: What is to order?

ZÜNDEL: Just so.

PSYCHIATRIST: Herr Zündel, we're here to help you.

ZÜNDEL: Yourself.

PSYCHIATRIST: You want to heal yourself?

ZÜNDEL: Heel, yourself.

PSYCHIATRIST: Let's show a little patience, eh, Herr Zündel.

ZÜNDEL: Fidelity is better.

PSYCHIATRIST: Do you hear voices, Herr Zündel?

ZÜNDEL: Fidelity is better.

PSYCHIATRIST: Better than what?

ZÜNDEL: Knickerbocker.

PSYCHIATRIST: Do you hear voices, Herr Zündel? Is someone speaking to you whom you can't see?

ZÜNDEL: I can see him!

PSYCHIATRIST: Whom do you see?

ZÜNDEL: Third at the back.

PSYCHIATRIST: Can you try and explain that to me.

ZÜNDEL: Barefoot. Desert humility.

PSYCHIATRIST: Herr Zündel, when is your birthday?

ZÜNDEL: Just now. Wrinkled.

PSYCHIATRIST: Who or what is wrinkled?

ZÜNDEL: Not recorded.
PSYCHIATRIST: Hmm, I see.
ZÜNDEL: Yes, going down.
PSYCHIATRIST: Hmm.
ZÜNDEL: Hunchbacked.
PSYCHIATRIST: Really?
ZÜNDEL: Satiated.
PSYCHIATRIST: Is that right?
ZÜNDEL: Upper homeland.
PSYCHIATRIST: Just carry on talking!
ZÜNDEL: Ssh!
PSYCHIATRIST: Do you hear anything?
ZÜNDEL: Ssh!

Dr. Läderach suggested schizophrenia.
    Dr. Hasler thought a depressive stupor.
    They agreed to keep the patient under observation.

24.

I visited him on August 8, a rainy Saturday. He seemed to know me, because when I walked in, he said: Sermon? – Yes, tomorrow! I said. – Be very careful, he whispered, the lambs! – Yes, Konrad, I said, moved.

Then we were quiet for a long time.

How are you feeling? I finally asked.

He said haltingly: The claws won't grow.

Give them time, I said, don't let it get you down!

Please, he said, abdicate, better now than in snowy drifts.

We have our lives to live, dear Konrad, I said, we can talk about abdicating in a few decades' time!

He asked: And what about the grief thistles?

They grow in gardens everywhere, I said.

And the wolves?

They're all God's creatures!

Amen! he exclaimed.

I creased my brow.

He said: Let them go to the bottom, fill them with stones and drop them at the bottom of the ocean, in Marianna's trench.

Erm, I said after a while, I have some bad news for you, Magda won't be able to visit you in the next few days. She was in excruciating pain last night, and was taken to hospital this morning. Acute appendicitis. They've already done the operation, and she sends her love. She's doing fine. Would you like me to take her a message?

Konrad sat there as though he had heard nothing. Finally he said: Don't believe it!

Don't believe what? I asked.

He said nothing, and seemed oblivious of my presence. His features looked delicate, almost translucent, like those of a dead man.

I left him to his reverie, and went away.

On Sunday morning, the head of the school visited him.

Take your time over getting better! he said to Zündel.

Replaced? asked Zündel.

Yes, answered the head, we've found a substitute teacher for you.

Tight, said Zündel, tight ship!

Oh, it's not so bad, said the head. Appearances deceive.

Rarely, said Zündel. And what's on the piece of paper?

What piece of paper?

The notice board, what does that say, what does that say about me?

It says "Absent until further notice," answered the head.

I see! cried Zündel, and his eyes lit up.

On Monday, his mother, Johanna, came to visit.

When she walked in, Konrad said: Lilith, begone!

Oh, my poor boy, wailed Johanna.

Zündel fled into a corner of the room, and whispered: False Madonna, you just lie under that atrabilious scoundrel, and I am the comeuppance, and I am the comeuppance, slap bang in the middle of January I am expelled from her belly.

Konrad, Konrad! exclaimed Johanna, but he turned quite pale, and would not say another word.

On Tuesday he didn't come down to supper.

His room was empty.

They couldn't find him in any of the day-rooms.

Fellow patients said they had seen him sitting on a park bench for hours, he had been wearing – in spite of the heat – a red and blue striped woolly hat. The duty doctor was censured by his superior, first informally, and two days later in writing.

The hospital porter likewise.

Magda was informed. From her hospital bed, she sent instructions that Zündel was not to be sought by the police or on the wireless. Was there any spot where she thought her husband might have gone?

There was a possibility that he might have gone to a weekend cottage near Hinwil. It belonged to his colleague Oswald Scholl who years ago had given Konrad a spare key.

Would she allow them to look for her husband there?

They could try, but she begged them to be gentle, he was not on any account to be forced to return.

Early on Wednesday morning, two burly auxiliary nurses – in the company of Scholl – set off to catch Zündel. They left their car in a field, and covered the last six or seven hundred yards on foot.

The shutters of the little wooden hut were thrown open. A ground floor window was open.

He was singing.

He was singing: Marble, stone and iron break, but not our love. Marble, stone and iron break, but not our love . . . Before Oswald could do anything to prevent it, one of the nurses banged on the door and yelled: Open up, police!

Are you mad? hissed Scholl.

A shot rang out.

The blundering nurse gave a jump.

The other dropped to the ground.

Zündel was standing in the window. His face was contorted, in his violently shaking hand he held a pistol.

Clear off, clear off! I have orders to shoot! he said gruffly.

Konrad, be sensible, we only want what's good for you, jabbered Oswald, as the two nurses scrambled for cover. Zündel said: Sensible my ass, go away, go away I tell you!

The three visitors hesitated, then Zündel raised his pistol and fired another shot. The bullet struck a tree. Fragments of bark were sprinkled over the heads of the intruders.

The nurses ran for it.

Oswald turned once more to give Konrad an uncertain and disbelieving look, and said: Forgive our appalling intervention, I'm going as well now, bye, look after yourself!

Sure, said Zündel, and closed the window.

(The provenance of the pistol, a 9 mm Smith & Wesson Parabellum, remains as much a mystery today as that of the woolly cap.)

Magda stuck to her guns: no violence! – The senior doctor understood her point of view, but had difficulty in defending it to the police. They had been notified by Mosimann, the aggressive auxiliary nurse, who consulted no one, and it was fortunate that they in turn, before they did anything, got in touch with the head doctor at the clinic.

Magda's suggestion was that, as Konrad's friend, I be sent to negotiate with him.

He accepts you, Magda said to me on the telephone, he won't hurt you, please look after him, I'm still too weak myself.

Since Oswald, whom I knew slightly through Konrad, wasn't free that Wednesday afternoon, his wife agreed to take me up to Hinwil and show me the hut, whose position she described to me in detail. She would wait down by the car.

Reverend, she said, Konrad always spooked me, I'm sure he was a nice fellow, but he was a bit prickly, you couldn't talk to him, please be careful, my husband thinks he's – right now anyway – unpredictable.

Yes, Frau Scholl, I replied, but he won't hurt me, we've known each other for almost twenty years now, I'm sure he'll feel my affection for him.

Oswald said something about a personality disorder, Frau Scholl replied shyly.

I can't really believe that, I said. But we'll see.

I too could hear him singing from a ways off, and was astonished by his clear, strong voice.

He was singing: Sing praise to the lord in the highest, for his compassion and truth . . . After "truth" he broke off, and began again. I stood beside the window. After a while he stopped singing. He said aloud: The old mutton pizzle is becoming churchy in his old days!

I stepped in front of the open window and spoke into the dark room: That would make me very happy, Konrad.

Only now, as he leapt up from the corner bench where he had been lying, did I see him. He was wearing his striped woolen cap and a knee-length cardigan.

Get back! he screamed, and grabbed the pistol on the table.

It's me, I said as calmly as I could. It's me, you remember, your friend Viktor.

Aggressively he said: I don't know anyone here, get away, I have orders to shoot.

The weapon was pointing straight at me.

I was afraid. His eyes were those of a stranger.

I said: Those orders might apply to your enemies, you'll surely not want to chase me away like a mangy dog.

Thereupon Konrad screamed at a terrifying volume: Leave me alone! Get lost.

Then he turned away, set the pistol down on the table, and stood there hunched and trembling.

Are you cold? I asked.

Of course, what do you think, he replied.

Come on then, let's have a drink, I said, I have a nice pinot from the Valais, you remember?

I took the bottle out of my briefcase and set it down on the windowsill.

Are they very badly hurt? he asked.

Who?

The policemen who were trying to capture me.

Not a bit of it, I said, they were a couple of orderlies from the clinic, they're both fine.

He said: Those goddamned loonies.

I went in, and sat down on a stool. – Konrad, I said, and I mean this: people really want the best for you.

In the pub, he said, in the pub I heard someone speaking at the next door table, a man of sixty-odd, with cigar and braces and a big square Swiss skull. And his friends looked like he did, and they agreed with him.

And what was he saying? I asked after a long pause.

He said he still felt gratitude to his late father for beating his bare behind three times a week with a cow's tail.

I see, I said.

That's right, he said, the perverts are in the pub, and people want to shut me in.

People want to look after you.

Ho ho, he said.

What about a glass, then? I asked him.

You should go now, he said, I'm not allowed to talk.

What do you have in mind, Konrad?

Desert or jungle or sea or sky, he replied.

Those were the last words I heard out of his mouth.

I said: All right, I'll go now, and I'll make sure no one comes and bothers you, neither the police nor the clinic.

No reply.

Magda sends her love, she'll come and see you as soon as she can, maybe as soon as tomorrow.

No reply.

Or do you want to come and stay with me for a couple of days? You could come and go as you please, and you know Vroni's always happy to see you!

A shake of the head.

I pointed to the pistol and asked: Do you mind if I take that?

He didn't react.

Slowly I reached for the weapon, and put it in my briefcase.

He watched, without putting up any fight.

All right, I said, bye bye, Konrad, don't give up, we love you and we need you. And remember: turn up any time of day or night, Vroni and I will always be happy to see you. – He looked at me. I squeezed his shoulder and went.

When Magda approached the hut the next evening (Thursday, August 13) on shaking legs – Oswald would have escorted her, but she made him stay in the car – Konrad was not singing. The door and window were ajar, Magda's calls found no echo.

She could sense right away that he wasn't there.

In the kitchen she found the woolly hat, and on a scrap of paper the words: Gone until further notice.

After four days of waiting, Magda conceded that it was pointless to stand in the way of the usual procedures: on August 18, the radio broadcast a missing person alert, and on the 19 Interpol were alerted.

In the middle of September, Hans Fischer wrote to Johanna Zündel from Vancouver, to say that Konrad had sent him a "large package" from Genoa, dated August 15. It contained a "trapezoidal lump of plaster of Paris" and "written materials" that made reference to "sundry difficulties and tendencies of his frail son."

Nothing more was heard of him.

Markus Werner was born in 1944 in Eschlikon, canton of Thurgau, Switzerland. Having written his dissertation on Max Frisch, Werner worked as a teacher in Schaffhausen before becoming a full-time writer in 1990. He is the author of seven novels, including *On the Edge* (2004), and has won numerous prizes.

Michael Hofmann is an award-winning poet, critic, and translator from German. Among his translations are works by Thomas Bernhard, Ernst Jünger, Franz Kafka, Wolfgang Koeppen, Joseph Roth, and his father, Gert Hofmann.

SWISS LITERATURE SERIES

In 2008, Pro Helvetia, the Swiss Arts Council, began working with Dalkey Archive Press to identify some of the greatest and most innovative authors in twentieth and twenty-first century Swiss letters, in the tradition of such world renowned writers as Max Frisch, Robert Walser, and Robert Pinget. Dalkey Archive editors met with critics and scholars in Zürich, Geneva, Basel, and Bern, and went on to prepare reports on numerous important Swiss authors whose work was deemed underrepresented in English. Developing from this ongoing collaboration, the Swiss Literature Series, launched in 2011 with Gerhard Meier's *Isle of the Dead* and Aglaja Veteranyi's *Why the Child Is Cooking in the Polenta*, has been working to remedy this dearth of Swiss writing in the Anglophone world with a bold initiative to publish four titles a year, each supplemented with marketing efforts far exceeding what publishers can normally provide for works in translation.

With writing originating from German, French, Italian, and Rhaeto-Romanic, the Swiss Literature Series will stand as a testimony to Switzerland's contribution to world literature.

MICHAL AJVAZ, *The Golden Age.*
The Other City.
PIERRE ALBERT-BIROT, *Grabinoulor.*
YUZ ALESHKOVSKY, *Kangaroo.*
FELIPE ALFAU, *Chromos.*
Locos.
IVAN ÂNGELO, *The Celebration.*
The Tower of Glass.
ANTÓNIO LOBO ANTUNES, *Knowledge of Hell.*
The Splendor of Portugal.
ALAIN ARIAS-MISSON, *Theatre of Incest.*
JOHN ASHBERY AND JAMES SCHUYLER, *A Nest of Ninnies.*
ROBERT ASHLEY, *Perfect Lives.*
GABRIELA AVIGUR-ROTEM, *Heatwave and Crazy Birds.*
DJUNA BARNES, *Ladies Almanack.*
Ryder.
JOHN BARTH, *LETTERS.*
Sabbatical.
DONALD BARTHELME, *The King.*
Paradise.
SVETISLAV BASARA, *Chinese Letter.*
MIQUEL BAUÇÀ, *The Siege in the Room.*
RENÉ BELLETTO, *Dying.*
MAREK BIEŃCZYK, *Transparency.*
ANDREI BITOV, *Pushkin House.*
ANDREJ BLATNIK, *You Do Understand.*
LOUIS PAUL BOON, *Chapel Road.*
My Little War.
Summer in Termuren.
ROGER BOYLAN, *Killoyle.*
IGNÁCIO DE LOYOLA BRANDÃO, *Anonymous Celebrity.*
Zero.
BONNIE BREMSER, *Troia: Mexican Memoirs.*
CHRISTINE BROOKE-ROSE, *Amalgamemnon.*
BRIGID BROPHY, *In Transit.*
GERALD L. BRUNS, *Modern Poetry and the Idea of Language.*
GABRIELLE BURTON, *Heartbreak Hotel.*
MICHEL BUTOR, *Degrees.*
Mobile.
G. CABRERA INFANTE, *Infante's Inferno.*
Three Trapped Tigers.
JULIETA CAMPOS, *The Fear of Losing Eurydice.*
ANNE CARSON, *Eros the Bittersweet.*
ORLY CASTEL-BLOOM, *Dolly City.*
LOUIS-FERDINAND CÉLINE, *Castle to Castle.*
Conversations with Professor Y.
London Bridge.
Normance.
North.
Rigadoon.
MARIE CHAIX, *The Laurels of Lake Constance.*
HUGO CHARTERIS, *The Tide Is Right.*
ERIC CHEVILLARD, *Demolishing Nisard.*

MARC CHOLODENKO, *Mordechai Schamz.*
JOSHUA COHEN, *Witz.*
EMILY HOLMES COLEMAN, *The Shutter of Snow.*
ROBERT COOVER, *A Night at the Movies.*
STANLEY CRAWFORD, *Log of the S.S. The Mrs Unguentine.*
Some Instructions to My Wife.
RENÉ CREVEL, *Putting My Foot in It.*
RALPH CUSACK, *Cadenza.*
NICHOLAS DELBANCO, *The Count of Concord.*
Sherbrookes.
NIGEL DENNIS, *Cards of Identity.*
PETER DIMOCK, *A Short Rhetoric for Leaving the Family.*
ARIEL DORFMAN, *Konfidenz.*
COLEMAN DOWELL,
Island People.
Too Much Flesh and Jabez.
ARKADII DRAGOMOSHCHENKO, *Dust.*
RIKKI DUCORNET, *The Complete Butcher's Tales.*
The Fountains of Neptune.
The Jade Cabinet.
Phosphor in Dreamland.
WILLIAM EASTLAKE, *The Bamboo Bed.*
Castle Keep.
Lyric of the Circle Heart.
JEAN ECHENOZ, *Chopin's Move.*
STANLEY ELKIN, *A Bad Man.*
Criers and Kibitzers, Kibitzers and Criers.
The Dick Gibson Show.
The Franchiser.
The Living End.
Mrs. Ted Bliss.
FRANÇOIS EMMANUEL, *Invitation to a Voyage.*
SALVADOR ESPRIU, *Ariadne in the Grotesque Labyrinth.*
LESLIE A. FIEDLER, *Love and Death in the American Novel.*
JUAN FILLOY, *Op Oloop.*
ANDY FITCH, *Pop Poetics.*
GUSTAVE FLAUBERT, *Bouvard and Pécuchet.*
KASS FLEISHER, *Talking out of School.*
FORD MADOX FORD,
The March of Literature.
JON FOSSE, *Aliss at the Fire.*
Melancholy.
MAX FRISCH, *I'm Not Stiller.*
Man in the Holocene.
CARLOS FUENTES, *Christopher Unborn.*
Distant Relations.
Terra Nostra.
Where the Air Is Clear.
TAKEHIKO FUKUNAGA, *Flowers of Grass.*
WILLIAM GADDIS, *J R.*
The Recognitions.

JANICE GALLOWAY, *Foreign Parts*.
  The Trick Is to Keep Breathing.
WILLIAM H. GASS, *Cartesian Sonata*
  and Other Novellas.
  Finding a Form.
  A Temple of Texts.
  The Tunnel.
  Willie Masters' Lonesome Wife.
GÉRARD GAVARRY, *Hoppla! 1 2 3*.
ETIENNE GILSON,
  The Arts of the Beautiful.
  Forms and Substances in the Arts.
C. S. GISCOMBE, *Giscome Road*.
  Here.
DOUGLAS GLOVER, *Bad News of the Heart*.
WITOLD GOMBROWICZ,
  A Kind of Testament.
PAULO EMÍLIO SALES GOMES, *P's Three
  Women*.
GEORGI GOSPODINOV, *Natural Novel*.
JUAN GOYTISOLO, *Count Julian*.
  Juan the Landless.
  Makbara.
  Marks of Identity.
HENRY GREEN, *Back*.
  Blindness.
  Concluding.
  Doting.
  Nothing.
JACK GREEN, *Fire the Bastards!*
JIŘÍ GRUŠA, *The Questionnaire*.
MELA HARTWIG, *Am I a Redundant
  Human Being?*
JOHN HAWKES, *The Passion Artist*.
  Whistlejacket.
ELIZABETH HEIGHWAY, ED., *Contemporary
  Georgian Fiction*.
ALEKSANDAR HEMON, ED.,
  Best European Fiction.
AIDAN HIGGINS, *Balcony of Europe*.
  Blind Man's Bluff
  Bornholm Night-Ferry.
  Flotsam and Jetsam.
  Langrishe, Go Down.
  Scenes from a Receding Past.
KEIZO HINO, *Isle of Dreams*.
KAZUSHI HOSAKA, *Plainsong*.
ALDOUS HUXLEY, *Antic Hay*.
  Crome Yellow.
  Point Counter Point.
  Those Barren Leaves.
  Time Must Have a Stop.
NAOYUKI II, *The Shadow of a Blue Cat*.
GERT JONKE, *The Distant Sound*.
  Geometric Regional Novel.
  Homage to Czerny.
  The System of Vienna.
JACQUES JOUET, *Mountain R*.
  Savage.
  Upstaged.

MIEKO KANAI, *The Word Book*.
YORAM KANIUK, *Life on Sandpaper*.
HUGH KENNER, *Flaubert*.
  Joyce and Beckett: The Stoic Comedians.
  Joyce's Voices.
DANILO KIŠ, *The Attic*.
  Garden, Ashes.
  The Lute and the Scars
  Psalm 44.
  A Tomb for Boris Davidovich.
ANITA KONKKA, *A Fool's Paradise*.
GEORGE KONRÁD, *The City Builder*.
TADEUSZ KONWICKI, *A Minor Apocalypse*.
  The Polish Complex.
MENIS KOUMANDAREAS, *Koula*.
ELAINE KRAF, *The Princess of 72nd Street*.
JIM KRUSOE, *Iceland*.
AYŞE KULIN, *Farewell: A Mansion in
  Occupied Istanbul*.
EMILIO LASCANO TEGUI, *On Elegance
  While Sleeping*.
ERIC LAURRENT, *Do Not Touch*.
VIOLETTE LEDUC, *La Bâtarde*.
EDOUARD LEVÉ, *Autoportrait*.
  Suicide.
MARIO LEVI, *Istanbul Was a Fairy Tale*.
DEBORAH LEVY, *Billy and Girl*.
JOSÉ LEZAMA LIMA, *Paradiso*.
ROSA LIKSOM, *Dark Paradise*.
OSMAN LINS, *Avalovara*.
  The Queen of the Prisons of Greece.
ALF MAC LOCHLAINN,
  The Corpus in the Library.
  Out of Focus.
RON LOEWINSOHN, *Magnetic Field(s)*.
MINA LOY, *Stories and Essays of Mina Loy*.
D. KEITH MANO, *Take Five*.
MICHELINE AHARONIAN MARCOM,
  The Mirror in the Well.
BEN MARCUS,
  The Age of Wire and String.
WALLACE MARKFIELD,
  Teitlebaum's Window.
  To an Early Grave.
DAVID MARKSON, *Reader's Block*.
  Wittgenstein's Mistress.
CAROLE MASO, *AVA*.
LADISLAV MATEJKA AND KRYSTYNA
  POMORSKA, EDS.,
  *Readings in Russian Poetics:
  Formalist and Structuralist Views*.
HARRY MATHEWS, *Cigarettes*.
  The Conversions.
  *The Human Country: New and
  Collected Stories*.
  The Journalist.
  My Life in CIA.
  Singular Pleasures.
  *The Sinking of the Odradek
  Stadium*.
  Tlooth.

JOSEPH MCELROY,
Night Soul and Other Stories.
ABDELWAHAB MEDDEB, Talismano.
GERHARD MEIER, Isle of the Dead.
HERMAN MELVILLE, The Confidence-Man.
AMANDA MICHALOPOULOU, I'd Like.
STEVEN MILLHAUSER, The Barnum Museum.
In the Penny Arcade.
RALPH J. MILLS, JR., Essays on Poetry.
MOMUS, The Book of Jokes.
CHRISTINE MONTALBETTI, The Origin of Man.
Western.
OLIVE MOORE, Spleen.
NICHOLAS MOSLEY, Accident.
Assassins.
Catastrophe Practice.
Experience and Religion.
A Garden of Trees.
Hopeful Monsters.
Imago Bird.
Impossible Object.
Inventing God.
Judith.
Look at the Dark.
Natalie Natalia.
Serpent.
Time at War.
WARREN MOTTE,
Fables of the Novel: French Fiction
since 1990.
Fiction Now: The French Novel in
the 21st Century.
Oulipo: A Primer of Potential
Literature.
GERALD MURNANE, Barley Patch.
Inland.
YVES NAVARRE, Our Share of Time.
Sweet Tooth.
DOROTHY NELSON, In Night's City.
Tar and Feathers.
ESHKOL NEVO, Homesick.
WILFRIDO D. NOLLEDO, But for the Lovers.
FLANN O'BRIEN, At Swim-Two-Birds.
The Best of Myles.
The Dalkey Archive.
The Hard Life.
The Poor Mouth.
The Third Policeman.
CLAUDE OLLIER, The Mise-en-Scène.
Wert and the Life Without End.
GIOVANNI ORELLI, Walaschek's Dream.
PATRIK OUŘEDNÍK, Europeana.
The Opportune Moment, 1855.
BORIS PAHOR, Necropolis.
FERNANDO DEL PASO, News from the
Empire.
Palinuro of Mexico.
ROBERT PINGET, The Inquisitory.
Mahu or The Material.
Trio.
MANUEL PUIG, Betrayed by Rita Hayworth.

The Buenos Aires Affair.
Heartbreak Tango.
RAYMOND QUENEAU, The Last Days.
Odile.
Pierrot Mon Ami.
Saint Glinglin.
ANN QUIN, Berg.
Passages.
Three.
Tripticks.
ISHMAEL REED, The Free-Lance Pallbearers.
The Last Days of Louisiana Red.
Ishmael Reed: The Plays.
Juice!
Reckless Eyeballing.
The Terrible Threes.
The Terrible Twos.
Yellow Back Radio Broke-Down.
JASIA REICHARDT, 15 Journeys Warsaw
to London.
NOËLLE REVAZ, With the Animals.
JOÃO UBALDO RIBEIRO, House of the
Fortunate Buddhas.
JEAN RICARDOU, Place Names.
RAINER MARIA RILKE, The Notebooks of
Malte Laurids Brigge.
JULIÁN RÍOS, The House of Ulysses.
Larva: A Midsummer Night's Babel.
Poundemonium.
Procession of Shadows.
AUGUSTO ROA BASTOS, I the Supreme.
DANIËL ROBBERECHTS, Arriving in Avignon.
JEAN ROLIN, The Explosion of the
Radiator Hose.
OLIVIER ROLIN, Hotel Crystal.
ALIX CLEO ROUBAUD, Alix's Journal.
JACQUES ROUBAUD, The Form of a
City Changes Faster, Alas, Than
the Human Heart.
The Great Fire of London.
Hortense in Exile.
Hortense Is Abducted.
The Loop.
Mathematics:
The Plurality of Worlds of Lewis.
The Princess Hoppy.
Some Thing Black.
RAYMOND ROUSSEL, Impressions of Africa.
VEDRANA RUDAN, Night.
STIG SÆTERBAKKEN, Siamese.
Self Control.
LYDIE SALVAYRE, The Company of Ghosts.
The Lecture.
The Power of Flies.
LUIS RAFAEL SÁNCHEZ,
Macho Camacho's Beat.
SEVERO SARDUY, Cobra & Maitreya.
NATHALIE SARRAUTE,
Do You Hear Them?
Martereau.
The Planetarium.

ARNO SCHMIDT, *Collected Novellas.*
Collected Stories.
Nobodaddy's Children.
Two Novels.
ASAF SCHURR, *Motti.*
GAIL SCOTT, *My Paris.*
DAMION SEARLS, *What We Were Doing*
and Where We Were Going.
JUNE AKERS SEESE,
Is This What Other Women Feel Too?
What Waiting Really Means.
BERNARD SHARE, *Inish.*
Transit.
VIKTOR SHKLOVSKY, *Bowstring.*
Knight's Move.
A Sentimental Journey:
Memoirs 1917–1922.
Energy of Delusion: A Book on Plot.
Literature and Cinematography.
Theory of Prose.
Third Factory.
Zoo, or Letters Not about Love.
PIERRE SINIAC, *The Collaborators.*
KJERSTI A. SKOMSVOLD, *The Faster I Walk,*
the Smaller I Am.
JOSEF ŠKVORECKÝ, *The Engineer of*
Human Souls.
GILBERT SORRENTINO,
Aberration of Starlight.
Blue Pastoral.
Crystal Vision.
Imaginative Qualities of Actual
Things.
Mulligan Stew.
Pack of Lies.
Red the Fiend.
The Sky Changes.
Something Said.
Splendide-Hôtel.
Steelwork.
Under the Shadow.
W. M. SPACKMAN, *The Complete Fiction.*
ANDRZEJ STASIUK, *Dukla.*
Fado.
GERTRUDE STEIN, *The Making of Americans.*
A Novel of Thank You.
LARS SVENDSEN, *A Philosophy of Evil.*
PIOTR SZEWC, *Annihilation.*
GONÇALO M. TAVARES, *Jerusalem.*
Joseph Walser's Machine.
Learning to Pray in the Age of
Technique.
LUCIAN DAN TEODOROVICI,
Our Circus Presents . . .
NIKANOR TERATOLOGEN, *Assisted Living.*
STEFAN THEMERSON, *Hobson's Island.*
The Mystery of the Sardine.
Tom Harris.
TAEKO TOMIOKA, *Building Waves.*

JOHN TOOMEY, *Sleepwalker.*
JEAN-PHILIPPE TOUSSAINT, *The Bathroom.*
Camera.
Monsieur.
Reticence.
Running Away.
Self-Portrait Abroad.
Television.
The Truth about Marie.
DUMITRU TSEPENEAG, *Hotel Europa.*
The Necessary Marriage.
Pigeon Post.
Vain Art of the Fugue.
ESTHER TUSQUETS, *Stranded.*
DUBRAVKA UGRESIC, *Lend Me Your*
Character.
Thank You for Not Reading.
TOR ULVEN, *Replacement.*
MATI UNT, *Brecht at Night.*
Diary of a Blood Donor.
Things in the Night.
ÁLVARO URIBE AND OLIVIA SEARS, EDS.,
Best of Contemporary Mexican Fiction.
ELOY URROZ, *Friction.*
The Obstacles.
LUISA VALENZUELA, *Dark Desires and*
the Others.
He Who Searches.
PAUL VERHAEGHEN, *Omega Minor.*
AGLAJA VETERANYI, *Why the Child Is*
Cooking in the Polenta.
BORIS VIAN, *Heartsnatcher.*
LLORENÇ VILLALONGA, *The Dolls' Room.*
TOOMAS VINT, *An Unending Landscape.*
ORNELA VORPSI, *The Country Where No*
One Ever Dies.
AUSTRYN WAINHOUSE, *Hedyphagetica.*
CURTIS WHITE, *America's Magic Mountain.*
The Idea of Home.
Memories of My Father Watching TV.
Requiem.
DIANE WILLIAMS, *Excitability:*
Selected Stories.
Romancer Erector.
DOUGLAS WOOLF, *Wall to Wall.*
Ya! & John-Juan.
JAY WRIGHT, *Polynomials and Pollen.*
The Presentable Art of Reading
Absence.
PHILIP WYLIE, *Generation of Vipers.*
MARGUERITE YOUNG, *Angel in the Forest.*
Miss MacIntosh, My Darling.
REYOUNG, *Unbabbling.*
VLADO ŽABOT, *The Succubus.*
ZORAN ŽIVKOVIĆ, *Hidden Camera.*
LOUIS ZUKOFSKY, *Collected Fiction.*
VITOMIL ZUPAN, *Minuet for Guitar.*
SCOTT ZWIREN, *God Head.*